THE SPINDLE

THE GRIMM STAR SAGA: FIRST LIGHT BOOK 2

J. DARLENE EVERLY

J. DARLENE EVERLY

THE SPINDLE

The Grimm Star Saga:
First Light Book 2

Hardcover: ISBN 978-1-954719-11-8
Paperback: ISBN 978-1-954719-10-1
Ebook: ISBN 978-1-954719-09-5
First paperback edition March 2021.
Edited by Beth Hale, Magnolia Editing.
Cover art by Jupiter Alley.
Layout by Wishing Well Books.

❀ Created with Vellum

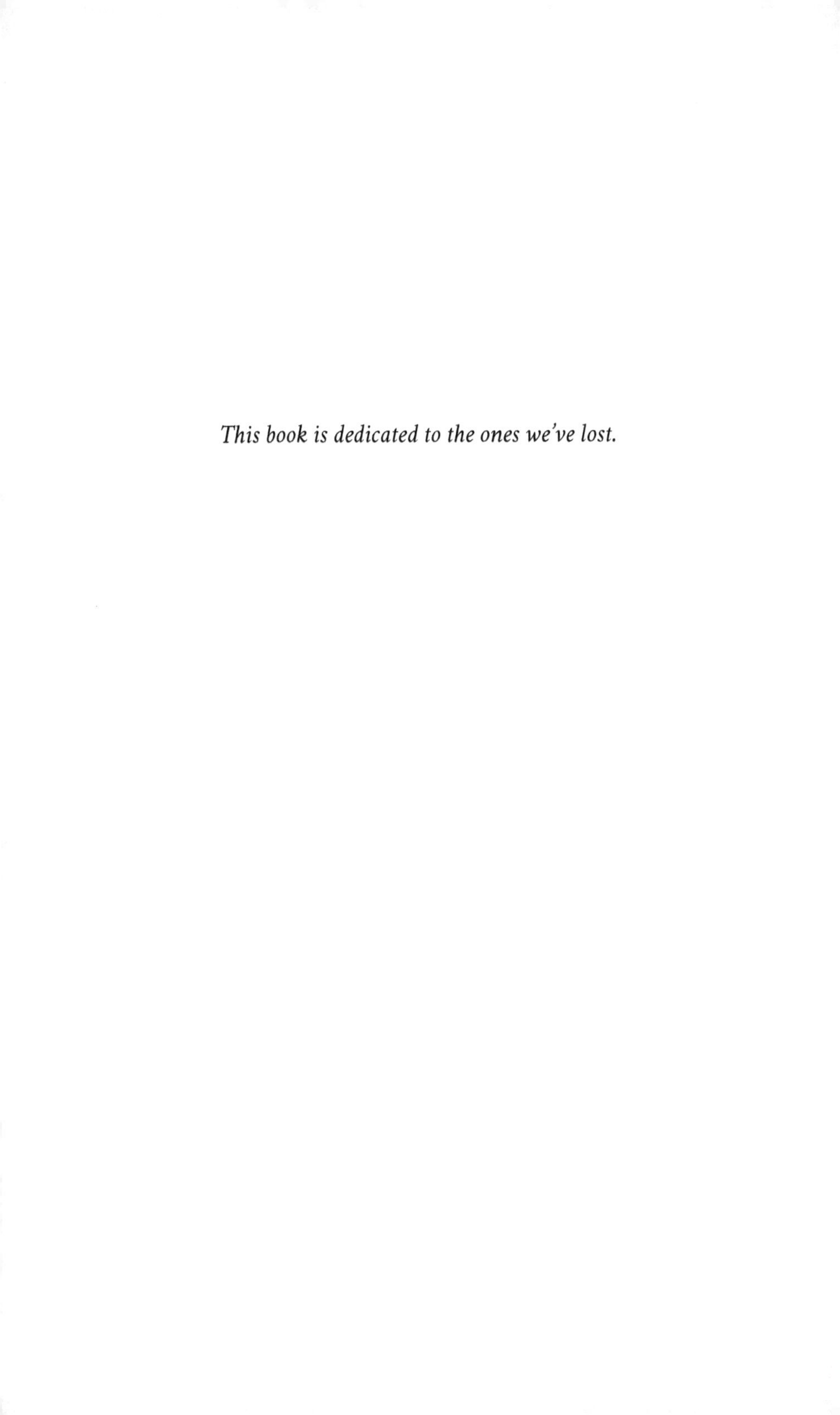

This book is dedicated to the ones we've lost.

ZELLENDINE

It took only seconds for it to rush back through Zellendine's mind. All of it. Troylus, the blue light as it poured from him, his lips on hers, the sleepers, Yanna and her baby, the horror of the Chapter computer, and Briar. Briar's eyes.

How much of his eyes were silver after an entire shift and almost one hundred years in stasis? Why had they started to turn? Why were Troylus's entirely silver?

While she probably should have been thinking about the nearness of the planet and the end of their journey, she couldn't. The only thing running through her mind was the vision of silver eyes. And she wasn't sure if they were Troylus's or what she imagined Briar's to look like.

She took deep breaths and stretched inside her cryo tube, barely managing to actually move. The first moments after waking from stasis were always unnerving to her in the best of times, but these were the most unnerving of times and she wanted simply to be able to get out of the damn tube faster than she knew was smart. It took time, turning her hands, flexing her fingers and curling them into fists. Time to roll her ankles around and breathe deeply.

The air tasted crisp with a tinge of stale, the cold still floated among the warmer air, and all of it had been locked away with her for one hundred years.

Her head spun if she spent too long thinking about the passage of time while she was in stasis. Instead, she wondered if she was going to have the time to figure out her plan of action after she landed. She wondered if she and Troylus would be able to warn the other Chapters of the computers, of the hideous truth.

She and Troylus... she stopped moving her arms for a second. They hung suspended above her while she realized she wasn't thinking about even trying to include Briar in her plans. She was thinking about Troylus.

While walking through the asteroid belt of the last shift, she and Troylus had become a team.

It made her smile. The smile was still playing on her lips as her tank opened and she managed to sit up. Directly in front of her, the large window looked out on the whole of their new sun. No mere wisps of solar flares, there she was in all her glory. Her smile grew wider.

Zellendine glanced to the left when a movement caught her eye. Her dad was levering himself up and seemed to be fine. Her smile was firmly in place as she turned to her right, looking past Rullon's hands stretching and flexing in the air, and she made eye contact with Troylus.

He was sitting in his tank with his knees drawn up and his arms resting atop them, looking right at her.

Troylus's face softened as he looked at her and his chest rose and fell on what she would have sworn was a sigh, but he didn't smile. He looked pained as he cut his eyes and gave the slightest of head nods in the direction of the tank behind him.

Zellendine tried to look past him, to the person sitting up in their tank and rubbing at their eyes as they flung their legs over the side far too soon.

When they stopped rubbing their eyes, Zellendine sucked in a breath, the smile dropping from her face.

Troylus nodded, once. He saw the silver first, the silver that had taken over one of their eyes. He was closer, but she had to wonder if his own change had alerted him in some way to the change of the person on his other side.

She wasn't even paying attention to who the person was because it didn't matter. The color of their eyes only mattered in that it confirmed for her what she suspected as she was going to sleep. Whatever had happened to Troylus was spreading.

But what was it? And what did it mean?

None of her questions had answers. At least none that she could think of.

Zellendine swung her legs over the side of her tank, she wanted to get to Briar in his cryo bay, she wanted to know how developed his change was.

"It's too early yet, Zellendine," Stephen said from his own tank.

"Don't worry, I'm still just stretching," she said, although she wanted to argue even though she knew he was right.

She bent over her legs and wiggled her toes, relishing in the tingling feeling that ran through her body as it came fully awake and back to the moment. She checked the display on the side of her tank, scrolling through the schedule for her check up in the clinic after waking. She was on the first day like medics usually were. And she checked what her assignment would be for her quarters. It was the same as she usually had.

Hmmm, she thought that every shift someone was assigned her quarters. If that were the case, what were the odds she would get the assignment of the same place she always had?

Maybe they had a different system. At least the Chapters got something right. She was happy to be assigned her own space.

Feet appeared below her, in the soft form slippers that they only wore for stasis.

Zellendine raised her head and found silver eyes no longer blocked by the slightly too long hair she missed, and a soft smile.

"You should sit," she said, placing a hand next to her on her tank. "No one wants you to fall down because you got up too soon."

He bit his bottom lip and perched next to her on the edge of the tank, gripping it with both hands and staring down at the floor.

She chewed on the inside of her cheek, hoping he knew that what she actually meant was that *she* didn't want him to fall down. For the few seconds he was in front of her she didn't care about anyone else or what they thought. But having him next to her instead, those silver eyes focused away from her, brought her mind reeling back to Briar and the other silver eyes that might be popping up around them.

"We'll be landing soon." Troylus kept his voice low and his expression smooth, but she thought she heard the worry in it.

"Yes, there will be a lot to plan and prepare for." There, that should be true enough generally that no one listening would think they were doing anything other than making small talk.

"As soon as I can, I want to spend some time with my sister. The orchard always helps me think a little more clearly about the planet and what I'll need to do once we land." Troylus inched his hand closer to hers along the edge of the tank and touched one knuckle against hers.

It was the tiniest amount of contact, but it still managed to make her heart pick up and her eyes dart around to check and see that no one noticed.

He was her friend, but he had also used their supposed estrangement to keep her out of trouble last shift. Would them having contact in front of people, against protocol unless they were partners or about to be partners, be enough to draw suspicion to her again?

Zellendine knew she couldn't afford the scrutiny, especially not if she was going to manage to implement her plan. But she couldn't force herself to move her hand away from his. No matter that it was the smart thing to do, Troylus managed to make her do all kinds of things that she would have said were objectively stupid. And she found herself appreciating it.

"Okay, that's a good idea, to think in the orchard. I wouldn't have thought of that." So, they were going to meet up in the orchard. She would haunt the place and be some kind of Zellendine-shaped fungus if she had to. If it meant stealing some time to talk to him and work through what their next move was, it would be worth it.

"The best time is usually when the night crew is on and everyone else is about to go to sleep. It's quiet then, the birds even settle down as the lights are dimmed," he said, his eyes meeting hers with a small smile on his face.

Well, it seemed she didn't have to turn into a fungus in the orchard after all.

Before she could think of another coded thing to say to him, a commotion at the end of the stacks of tanks drew her attention.

A couple stasis crew members ran by the end of the stacks toward the noise of grunting and incoherent yelling.

The last time there was something out of the ordinary while people were coming out of stasis, Upton and the other sleepers were trapped in REM sleep.

"Not again," Zellendine said, her voice a gush of air as her head spun with the possibilities and a chill ran up her spine. It was why she had looked back. The fear of it happening again, she wasn't sure what she was going to do if the sleeping was a problem again. Would everyone expect her to be able to wake them in an instant? How would she cover for the fact that it was Troylus, his blue light, that freed them?

She looked over at Troylus, meeting his eyes and seeing some of the same questions playing there in his gaze. What she didn't expect was the way his eyes snuck a peek at her lips, it made heat rise in her cheeks and she dropped her eyes from his.

If they needed to wake more people, would it mean she needed to kiss Troylus again? She wasn't sure why that thought made her smile. She tried to hide her grin in a grimace as she pushed herself up to stand on legs that wanted to buckle under her.

Troylus slipped one hand around her waist and held her elbow with the other, seeming to be unbothered by the stasis drag. As glad as she was to have him there to help her walk, his nearness after thinking about their kiss didn't help steady her legs.

Rounding the end of the stack, they met up with Stephen who was taking tiny steps by hanging onto the stack next to him and heading in the same direction they were.

They didn't have to go far before they discovered the origin of the sounds. It was a problem for sure, but it was about as opposite a problem from the sleepers as it could be.

2

TROYLUS

What the hell? Troylus thought as he stared at the two people trying, and mostly failing, to pummel each other with their fists. One of them was far more coordinated than the other, but neither was anything nearing graceful and often landed blows on the floor or stack nearest them rather than their opponent.

"That is the weirdest way to wake up I've ever seen," Troylus said and Zellendine snorted before suppressing the rest of the laugh he could feel in her waist.

"Stop it. This is messed up," she said, but there was no anger in her voice at all. In fact, he could have sworn she leaned just a bit closer to him.

Go ahead and fight, he wanted to say. If it got Zellendine past the stupid protocols and helped get her over the initial awkwardness after they woke up, he was fine with a couple dipshits fighting.

It took multiple attempts for the two stasis crew members who responded to the fight to pull the combatants apart.

Stephen caught up to Troylus and Zellendine and leaned against the end of the stack, shaking his head.

"How can they have anything to be angry enough to fight about? They just woke up," Stephen asked.

Troylus looked back at the people on the ground, their ridiculous battle aside, he might have an idea of how they could be mad enough to risk being denied entry to the planet for a short-lived fight.

Sure enough, when they were pulled apart one of them had silver eyes and the other had regular blue eyes.

He looked at Zellendine, her dark eyes were wide and the fear in them made him want to hide her away from everyone and beat the crap out of himself. She understood the anger that the silver eyed person felt because he had directed the same at her. The blue eyed person was just protecting themselves from an attack, just like Zellendine would have had to do if Troylus had not been so careful not to let it get that far and to overcome the wrath he recognized as irrational.

"It doesn't matter how many, it won't happen to you again," Troylus whispered to her, hoping that Stephen didn't hear him as he pulled himself along the end of the stacks to look over the two fighters for any injuries. Troylus kept Zellendine as far from the silver-eyed person as he could, her dad could handle it. Stephen was always a medic first, but Zellendine was more scared than medic right now, and Troylus could not blame her.

"Maybe I should just go to quarters and wait for my dad there," she whispered back.

"Come on," he said, leading her around the groups on the floor and toward the door. Stephen and Rullon would both be fine. They had been through enough shifts to take their time and find them when they could.

But they had taken too long. Some people were already up and moving through the halls to get to their own destinations after waking. The corridor outside the cryo bay was more crowded than Troylus had ever seen it.

"Not everyone wakes at exactly the same time?" Zellendine asked, breathless, next to him, slumping against his side.

"I guess not, but we'll be fine," he said, pulling her closer and lacing her fingers with his. He didn't do it just to support her, nothing in his life had prepared him to be so surrounded by people he didn't know.

But Troylus looked down at Zellendine and gave her a smile, trying for reassuring, and he must have landed somewhere near it because she smiled back before he stepped with her into the flow of humanity.

They tried not to bump into the people around them, they tried not to step on anyone's feet and give everyone the distance they were used to. It didn't work.

"Ouch," Zellendine said and Troylus whipped his head around to the person next to her who gave a chagrined sorry before moving off down an off shoot of the main hallway.

"Are you okay?" he asked.

"Yeah. He just stepped on my foot." She squeezed his hand, and he loosened his grip on her, realizing he was holding on too tight.

"Somehow I never thought about how small this ship would seem when we were all awake." He wanted the landing to be the next day, waiting through this kind of crowding might make him a ball of blue rage again and no one wanted that.

"Do you think I'll be sharing my quarters with anyone who, um..." Zellendine trailed off and he couldn't find a way to say what he knew she meant so instead he answered.

"No. And if you are, I'll talk them into switching with me and Rullon." It might not have been the truth. He couldn't guess what her new roommates would agree to, but it was what he hoped would happen.

"That would be, um, interesting. Sharing quarters with you," she said, ducking her head so he couldn't see her face.

"More interesting than sharing with a stranger?" he asked, genuinely curious. To him it made more sense to be comfortable with people you knew than living in the same tiny space as people you didn't.

"Well…" she trailed off and bit her lip, casting her eyes at the floor.

"Zellendine?" he asked, his voice low and soft. He wasn't sure why she fumbled over the answer, but something about her reaction sent his heart pounding in his chest.

"Look," she said, holding her head up and looking at him. She squared her shoulders, which made him wonder if he did something wrong.

"Troylus? Zellendine?" Briar asked near them, his voice sharp and higher than usual.

Damn it, Troylus thought. He was going to have to pass helping Zellendine over to Briar, but he sure as hell didn't want to.

"Hey, Briar," Troylus said, stopping, as tucked against the wall as he could make himself be, pulling Zellendine out of the flow of people so they could talk to his friend.

"What's this?" Briar's voice shot out as he gestured to where they held hands.

"A fight broke out in the cryo bay and I didn't want to be around it even though I'm not very steady yet, so Troylus was helping me to my quarters. I thought everyone was waking up at the same time," Zellendine said. Briar's eyes narrowed as she spoke, and it took Troylus a second longer than it should have to notice anything other than Zellendine's grip growing tighter on his.

"Of course, you caused a fight by being a bitch first thing

after waking up." Briar's words were like knives, Zellendine physically recoiling as each one hit.

Troylus snapped his shocked gaze back to Briar's completely silver eyes.

Shit. His stomach filled with a weight like when he was entering the gravity of the ship after a walk.

"No, Briar, she didn't do anything wrong. I think you know that. You can figure it out," Troylus said, biting back the ugly words he wanted to throw at him only because he knew Zellendine would be happier if Briar could get past the irrational rage like he had.

"Fuck you, Troylus. Stay out of this." Briar stepped closer to Zellendine. He loomed over her even though he wasn't taller that she was. His rage was so big it made him seem larger, and his muscles were poised like he was about to attack.

Troylus jerked her back and tucked her behind his own body. There was no damn way he was about to stand by while that happened.

"Damn it, I said stay out of it." Briar flung his arms out and connected with someone passing by.

"Oof," they said, their regular green eyes narrowed and a sneer formed on their face. "Watch it."

"You were in my way. You don't get to talk to me like that," Briar yelled, turning his wrath on the poor random person whose sneer left their face in a second as they backed up, their hands out in front of them.

"Can you walk?" Troylus whispered to Zellendine.

"I'm fine now," Zellendine said, but she still leaned against the wall and grabbed at his uniform. "Don't do it. Stay as far away as you can from whatever fight they're about to start. If you get in a fight too, leadership could come down on you. You could lose the chance to go to the planet."

Her face was pinched and her gaze was hard, like she was trying to will him not to step in.

"I can't just let Briar get ruined by this either. He might be barred from going to the planet too. I know you want him there with you. Trust me," he said, pulling her hand away from his uniform and stepping between Briar and the hapless passerby.

3

ZELLENDINE

SSHE TOOK A STEP TOWARD THEM, REACHING OUT TO SNATCH Troylus back, but bodies moved and blocked her.

People all around them were stopping and gawking, some even yelling, trying to egg them on. What was wrong with everyone?

Zellendine tried to see, ducking down to look around the people in front of her. She couldn't tell what they were saying to each other, but the random stranger finally turned to walk away while Briar pushed and shoved at Troylus who managed to stop him from going after the person. Her heart and her breathing were ragged as she tried to figure out what she would do to stop them from being kept off the planet.

Finally, Briar pointed a finger in Troylus's face and yelled something before he turned on his heel and walked away.

Troylus rubbed his face with one hand and turned to spot her in the crowd.

In front of her, the person blocking her view turned to face her.

Silver eyes flashed before he snarled an unintelligible string of pure rage and lashed out with a hand, connecting with the arm she raised to block him from getting to her face.

Her balance was still not perfect, the blow sent her toppling onto the floor of the hall.

Above her, Troylus shoved the man so hard he crashed into the wall and slumped over, holding his head while blood poured from his nose.

The people in the hallway looked on, shock and fear on so many strangers faces.

Zellendine allowed Troylus to pull her to her feet and hustled with him down the hall to the next branch of corridor.

She needed to go straight to her quarters, but her mind was flying trying to find a way to keep Troylus away from everyone until she knew how much trouble he was in.

"Go to the orchard," she said, shoving him toward the turn in the corridor, away from her path.

"Why? I need to stay with you," he said, raising his brow, a look full of warning and concern on his face.

"I can get to my quarters without another run in. You need to go to the orchard and hide until I can make sure you're not going to take the fall for all of that." She shoved at him again, whipping her head back and forth, scanning the faces of the people walking the hall, looking for any sign of the leadership coming for him.

Troylus looked around him then and wilted.

"Fine, but come and get me as soon as you can. I don't trust any of these people not to try and hurt you again." He grabbed her hand and squeezed it before he turned and made his way toward the only place she could think might be less crowded onboard.

She took a second to lean against the wall, taking deep breaths, and trying not to assume that everything was going to shit mere minutes after she woke up.

Okay, she told herself, get to quarters, and get someone to help.

At least she had a plan. Although the very thought of trusting anyone with the absolutely nonsense things that had happened, even though they were real, nauseated her. But she knew she couldn't figure out what was happening to everyone on her own.

There were only two people she thought might believe her, and only one she thought would be able to help her try and come up with an answer to why. Let alone how to stop it in time for them to land and make it work on the planet.

Of all the things the Chapter was wrong about, she still believed that they would need all the people on the ship, the expertise and skills of all the different people and their different roles, to make a whole new civilization work.

She had spent her entire life on board the Wheel, but at least some of the population remembered what it was like on a planet. She didn't think they would make it without those people. If some of them were turning silver, if some of them started attacking those who didn't have silver eyes, how long would it take before they were left far too weakened to make a new life on the planet?

A shudder ran down her back as she finally reached the door to her quarters.

Opening the door, she had a moment to wonder if she should knock first. She and her dad would be sharing their quarters, she had to remember that and act accordingly.

But, for now, the only person inside was her dad, eating a bar at the table.

Zellendine crossed the room to the table, feeling each step, the awakening and strengthening of her muscles that carried with it the kind of fatigue that always followed coming out of stasis. No matter how tired she was, she had to sit up straight and face her dad. She had to tell him the truth and hope he would believe her and help.

"I don't know what is going on with people right now, it has to be something about the crowds, but I think you should spend as little time as possible in the halls." Stephen shook his head as he popped the last bite of his bar in his mouth.

"The crowds sure don't help," she said, biting the inside of her cheek and willing herself to continue. But he beat her to it.

"After the cryo bay I saw another exchange, barely even that, almost turn into a fight in the hallway. I thought you would have beat me here."

He got up from the table and puttered around the server, frowning at the meager offerings, before he decided on a drink.

"Troylus and I had our own run in with fights in the halls," she said, wondering which direction he went. He probably stopped by the clinic. That would explain how she had missed him — he came from the opposite way.

"You did? Are you okay?" He turned and narrowed his eyes, examining her for any sign of injury.

She waved a hand at him and shook her head.

"I'm fine. But it's a bit more complicated than that."

A line formed between his brows and he took his seat across from her again, folding his arms on top of the table and giving her every bit of his attention.

Licking her lips, she told him everything he didn't already know. Including the kiss and the way the sleepers had really been saved. His face changed a fraction at a time, but by the time she was finished explaining about the fights in the hall and where Troylus was, his mouth hung slightly open, his eyes were wide, and he seemed to be looking through her.

Zellendine waited, her hands clenching and unclenching in her lap, while she hoped he would believe her and have some idea of how to help her figure it all out.

"Where is Troylus? The orchard?" he asked, shaking his head, his face returning to animation as he stood up from the table.

"Yes, but do you think it's okay to go to him? What about leadership?" she asked, pushing herself to standing although she felt her body dragging and not wanting to do as she asked.

"Leadership will be plenty busy with all of these fights. I doubt he'll even be questioned. Besides, he only hit the person after they hit you. I don't see how they could have a problem with that. If they do, I'll make sure nothing comes of it." He ushered her back out into the mass of people streaming down the hallway.

This time she followed close in his wake and tried even harder not to touch any of the people she passed.

Without Troylus there with them, she was worried both she and her dad would be targets.

But they only passed one argument on the way, and that was being broken up by others, so they didn't stop to intervene.

Stephen would normally be the first person to try and make something like that better, but maybe her warnings about why they were happening had changed his mind. She sure hoped so. The last thing she wanted was for him to be hurt in all of this, but she was worried about everyone being hurt by each other over something none of them even understood, let alone could stop from happening.

Making the last turn to the orchard, she missed a step and had to focus on just walking to keep going. What tripped her up was the realization that Troylus had managed to overcome whatever it was that caused the silver eyed people to rage at those around them.

Her dad stopped, steps into the orchard, looking around.

"Come on, I know where he is," she said, walking into the trees.

4

TROYLUS

He should have been able to fall asleep. In the past, the first three days after coming out of cryo were all struggles just to stay awake. But now... it was more than the stress. It was more than the thousand questions running through his brain.

Troylus rubbed his hands over his face, a rough gesture that only woke him up more, and stared upward at the branches of the tree he watched the birds in.

It was stupid for him to hope that other birds would be in the same tree, but he had. And they weren't.

Somewhere, not too far from where he lay sprawled on the ground, he heard a quick trill of one of the bird's voices.

At least that, and the rest of the orchard around him, felt like it wasn't shifting so fast he couldn't keep up with the flags coming at him. If he shut his eyes, he could even convince himself that the same nest would be above him on the branch when he opened them again.

Footsteps, light but shuffling, sounded on the dirt near him and he popped open his eyes, trying to figure out if he should stay as still as possible and hope whoever it was didn't notice him, or if he should try and hide.

But through the trees, he spotted the shine of blonde hair and let out his breath in a whoosh. Zellendine.

She should have been getting some food and some rest. They were supposed to take it easy when they first woke up. She had run headlong into a maelstrom of stress and even been hit. How she was still on her feet and coming to him, he didn't know.

But there she was, rounding a tree trunk and smiling as her shoulders relaxed.

Maybe he should have sat up, instead of remaining prone on the ground with a goofy grin on his face, maybe he would have if she had hinted at all that her dad was right behind her.

As soon as he spotted Stephen, Troylus scrambled to sit up and put his face back to his regular look of indifference. But she had surprised him and he wasn't so sure he was hiding it well.

"I wasn't expecting you," he said, kicking himself that it sounded like an accusation.

"Why not?" Zellendine asked, taking a seat at his side. "I wasn't going to just leave you here all night. You need to get some rest."

He hmmphed, thinking that she needed it more than he did.

"Troylus," she said, stretching a hand out like she was going to place it on his knee and then pulling it back to her lap. "I told Stephen."

Of all the things he thought she was going to say to explain her dad's presence, that wasn't one of them. And what, exactly, had she told him?

"Everything." Her voice was hushed and the gravity of Stephen, a member of leadership, knowing every secret he and Zellendine were keeping made his heart stutter in his chest.

Stephen took a seat on his other side, looking deep into his eyes. Which would have been weird on its own, but the look Stephen had while he did it was like he was studying Troylus. Like Troylus was some kind of sample in front of him in the clinic.

"For your professional opinion?" Troylus asked Stephen, who shook his head and gave him a rueful smile before he settled back to a less clinical stance.

"Yes, in a way. Before we try and tackle the plan you two have come up with to deal with the computers," Stephen said, looking between him and Zellendine while his brows knit together and relaxed again, "I want to run a quick scan of you so I might be able to figure out what is happening to everyone."

"What about leadership? Shouldn't you be telling them everything?" Troylus asked, trying not to sound angry and failing. She could have talked to him about bringing her dad into this.

"Maybe, but I don't tell them a lot of what goes on in the clinic. Until I need to tell them something, until we have something to tell them, I'm going to consider this a personal medical matter."

Troylus looked to Zellendine, who did reach out to place a barely there touch on his knee.

He blew out his breath then squeezed his lips together at the open and trusting look on her face.

"You think I should do this?" he asked, the bitter tone finally gone, he realized that now he sounded scared. Which... he was.

"Of all the people on this ship that we can trust, my dad and yours are the only people I think we should try to. I don't even know where to start," she said, dropping her hand back into her lap and following it with her eyes.

Good job, asshole, he told himself, you made her feel bad.

"Alright." He had to stop himself from smiling when her head snapped back up and she looked at him, her face full of hope and determination. He had seen it before when she was on a mission to wake the sleepers.

"How long should I hang out here? When will you find out from leadership if I'm going to get in trouble for all of this?" He swallowed, and tried to pretend that he wasn't worried he would never get to see the planet, that he wasn't hoping he wouldn't end up in the same kind of trial that Zellendine was in. Would she testify for him? Would that ploy work a second time?

Stephen just smiled and stood up, brushing off his pants.

"Don't worry about leadership. There were so many fights, they won't be able to discipline everyone, and I'm going to tell them you were protecting someone else." Stephen turned and walked to the edge of the little clearing before he turned back around. "Are you two coming, or not?"

Zellendine got up and pulled him to his feet while her father disappeared into the trees.

"What are we doing right now? Because I think I missed something," Troylus said, still stuck on the fact that Stephen just said he was going to defend him with leadership.

"Just come to the clinic with us real quick and then we're all going to finally get some sleep," Zellendine said, slipping her arm through his and leaning on him as they walked.

"Are you exhausted? You could go to quarters now, you don't have to stay with me," he said, his voice low and even although he didn't feel even. He wanted her to stay with him as long as possible, but she needed sleep.

"No," she said, laughing, "I mean, yes. I am tired, but no, I'm staying." She bumped him in the side with her elbow and he managed to suppress a toothy smile into just a grin.

"So, have you changed your mind about the quarters assignments after you've met your new roommates?" His grin fell from his lips with the words. Whoever she would be sharing a room with might not be someone who would want to hurt her, but he also didn't want it to be someone who would fall for her either. It was bad enough for Briar and her to be together and he had to deal with his jealousy and bitterness about that, he wasn't sure he would be able to not be an asshole if there was another one.

"Are you a little green?" she asked, a smug smile on her face.

"Of course I'm jealous. You're going to partner with Briar, someone else gets to spend a bunch of time with you away from crowds, and the whole time all I get to do is worry that someone is going to attack you again."

Zellendine pulled her arm from his and turned the corner into the steady stream of people in the hall, leaving him to trail behind her.

Well, that level of honesty sure as shit didn't work. Maybe he should have told her he wasn't jealous at all. But she would have seen the truth through an obvious lie. At least, he thought she would. He thought she understood exactly how he felt.

Maybe she just wasn't ready to handle that.

5

ZELLENDINE

Troylus just had to drop all pretense of talking about fun other things and throw a big black hole into the middle of their conversation. He was so damn serious, and she could barely keep focused on the importance of not bumping into the strangers all around her. How did he expect her to be able to respond coherently?

Was she just supposed to admit that she wasn't sure she wanted to partner with Briar anymore and she wasn't going to unless she was sure? Part of her wanted to tell Troylus that, but most of her was afraid he wouldn't just let that be enough. And she wasn't one hundred percent sure she wanted more with him either.

How had everything grown so complicated? It was supposed to get simpler on the planet, but she was starting to doubt that would be the case. For now, all she could do was keep her focus on this next problem, this next step. And try not to trip and fall.

People were everywhere in the hall. Their constant presence made the walk take longer than it ever had before. Finally, they reached the clinic and walking in the door to the familiar space allowed her to take a deep breath.

Usually, there weren't people waiting at this hour. During regular shifts, someone would only be on duty in case they were needed. Now, every seat in the front was full and there was a general hum from the exam rooms surrounding the center as if most of them were full.

Zellendine started to reach for Troylus's hand, looking for an anchor in all the differences around her. At the last second, she pulled it back to her side. Even though she knew no one around her, it wouldn't be smart to break protocol in front of them. She would have to remind herself of the near constant nature of eyes now that everyone was awake.

Stephen popped his head out of a doorway and waved them forward, Zellendine saw at least one person look irritated that they were called back after just getting there. But no one knew what the medics really did unless they were assigned to a medic crew, so they didn't voice their complaint.

"Is it going to be like this until we land?" Troylus asked, his voice tinged with a growl as he shut the door behind him.

"Like what?" Stephen asked, tapping away at a holo and getting the supplies he needed together.

"He means the overcrowding," Zellendine said, earning her a look and raised eyebrows from Troylus. She gave him a small smile and shrugged. Yes, she did understand at least that much of what he was thinking.

"Oh, well, yes. It was always going to be tight for this month while everyone is awake. Which is part of why I'm looking forward to the reports from terraforming on how long they think they'll need to work before we will all be able to land." Stephen turned back to them and smiled at each of them.

"You think we might have to spend more time on board waiting?" Zellendine didn't want that to be the case, how many more people were going to get into fights with everyone squished together, impatient, and whatever trigger was happening to the people with the silver eyes.

"It's possible, but it will probably just be you and me waiting. Troylus here will be one of the first people to step foot on our planet." Stephen was in medic mode, tapping his holo and attaching scanners to Troylus's hand.

Zellendine knew it was a possibility that a year would pass between the first Spindle landing on the planet and when the rest of the Spindles would transport the majority of the population to the ground. But her mind managed to suppress the idea of an entire shift away from Troylus until right that moment.

Troylus bit his lip and furrowed his brow, turning to stare at the wall instead of looking anywhere near her face. She wasn't sure what that meant about his feelings on the possibility. She was going to have to ask him.

A lump formed in her throat.

Stephen stepped back from Troylus, his eyes never leaving his holo as he tapped out commands and his face grew increasingly pinched.

"Will that thing really tell you what caused this?" Troylus asked, waving a hand toward the medic holo.

"Hmmm," Stephen muttered, not answering his question and making the lump in Zellendine's throat drop into her stomach.

"Is that noise bad?" Troylus asked, leaning forward and finally making eye contact with Zellendine while she tried to make her face as impassive as possible.

"Dad?" she asked, not wanting to play the protocol name game and waste time as he was more likely to respond if she didn't call him Stephen. Sure enough, he popped his head up and looked back and forth between her and Troylus.

"Ah, I'm sorry. I was too focused. I'm not sure yet if the readings will tell me the cause, but they might. For now, all I can say is that it is very clear this isn't just your eyes anymore."

Troylus's eyebrows shot up and his mouth worked like he was trying to say something, and the words failed him.

Zellendine wanted to sit in the chair behind her, to allow her legs to just give out. Instead, she stepped to Troylus's side, slipping her hand into his.

"What do you mean it isn't just his eyes?" she asked. Her voice was quiet, but it jolted Troylus. He jumped and squeezed her hand while he shut his eyes.

Stephen raised his eyes and paused his tapping, looking at them both in shock, "I'm sorry, I didn't mean to scare you. You're okay."

Troylus slumped into her side and Zellendine leaned back against him dragging a harsh breath into her lungs.

"What I mean is that there is now a silver line around every one of your blood cells and I can see that there is a new line of DNA here that didn't exist there before," Stephen said, turning the holo so Zellendine and Troylus could see it, although she didn't think he knew what any of the charts on it meant.

"If my DNA is all the sudden different, what does that mean health wise for the future?" Troylus asked, looking at the holo like he would find the answer to all the questions in the universe within it.

"Actually, this seems to improve your chances for good health long term, your telomeres are longer than they used to be." Stephen tapped at the holo and the image of the lengthened telomere was clear side by side with the image of his old one.

"Zellendine?" Troylus asked, looking to her with a nod of his head toward the holo.

"They can be seen as one of the markers suggesting a long life. The longer they are, the longer a person often lives," she said, her voice weak as she tried to imagine what his extraordinarily long ones would equate to in years.

"Oh, okay." He relaxed a bit and then tilted his head to the side studying her. "What's the matter?"

"Nothing," she said, too fast. Her answer was too fast and too dismissive, she knew it by the narrowing of his eyes and the thinning line of his mouth.

"Stephen," she said, maybe she could distract him, and herself, by barreling ahead, "You said there's a whole new section of DNA? How is that possible?"

"That I don't have an answer to yet. I need to spend some time with this information, to check all of it and compare it to the base readings for him." He stopped to yawn, his jaw popping it opened so large.

Zellendine yawned back, and Troylus put a hand to his mouth like he was fighting off one of his own.

"First, I think we need to head to quarters and get some rest," Stephen said.

She waited until Troylus nodded to agree herself. If he wanted more answers right at that second, she would have argued for it on his behalf. This was his genetic makeup, his confusing ability and changed anatomy. She wasn't going to try and tell him it wasn't important, but he seemed to be lost in his head over what they had already learned. But maybe, she thought, that was projection on her part.

6

TROYLUS

He wasn't sure which was worse, the fact that he was so
fundamentally changed when he didn't feel any different, or the
fact that Zellendine seemed unnerved by all of it.

But he knew he didn't trust any of the people on board to
not be set off simply by her being around just like he used to be.
Her touch, comforting as it was, still sent his blood hotter
through his veins. He still had a physiological reaction to her
presence, like she was a sun and he was a planet in her orbit.

Part of him wanted to know if he would feel anything like
that without the changes, but he enjoyed it too much to wish it
away. As hard as it was at first, as much as he had raged at her
because of it in the beginning of his changing eyes, now it was
one of the best things about his life.

"Stephen," Troylus said as they exited the clinic, Zellendine's
steps slowing next to him as she wilted under the exhaustion of
coming out of stasis, "I'm going to go with you both to your
quarters just to make sure neither of you fall asleep in the
hallway."

"I'm not going to fall asleep," Zellendine said, managing to sound more awake when she was indignant than she had before.

He grinned while Stephen gave a soft smile.

"That's appreciated, Troylus. Are you sure you will have no trouble returning to your own quarters?" He stepped forward, leading them so other people could pass, but he tilted his head a bit so Troylus knew he was still listening.

"Yes. I don't know if it's part of all of this, but I am less tired right now than I think I ever have been right after waking up." He shook his head. That didn't make any sense, but it was the truth, and another sign that none of this was normal.

"Okay, well, if you need help, the stasis crew should be available to get you to your quarters." Stephen faced entirely forward then, his feet slowing just a bit more.

Zellendine dropped a step behind, her blinks growing longer.

"Nope," Troylus said, scooping an arm behind her back and picking her up to pull her closer to him.

She let out a quick, sharp yipe sound.

"Put me down." Her voice was a whisper, but it was weighted, like it was made of metal.

"I am not going to let you fall asleep, or fall behind, especially when it seems like there are more silver eyed people wanting to kill you by the minute." Troylus answered her with the same steel in his hushed words.

"Fine," she said, stomping forward, getting in front of him and almost catching up with her dad.

Good. A pissed off Zellendine was a safer Zellendine, and that was all he cared about.

They finally reached their quarters and Troylus realized he hadn't planned this far ahead. He wasn't sure how to say 'see you later' when he didn't want to. They would never have to go into stasis again. He would never have to think about the reality of being away from her for one hundred years again. Yet they only had a month before he was leaving for the planet, a month that could be followed by a year apart. A year he would feel every second of if they were apart.

It felt cruel. Time was cruel.

Stephen opened the door, looked back at Troylus, and said, "I'll look through all of this and get it back to you," before he went inside, leaving the door open wide.

Two people were asleep in the bunks, their shoes lined up at the foot of the beds.

"Well," Troylus said, rubbing the back of his neck and wondering why he was suddenly far more uncomfortable than he had been. "If you have any issues with your new bunk mates, like I said, the offer still stands. I'm sure you're fine for tonight, but in the morning."

He rambled. His mouth wanted to be moving, but it sure as hell didn't want to be talking. He couldn't bring himself to speak normally. What an idiot. Okay, shut up, he told his brain, barely managing not to say it out loud.

"I'll keep that in mind," she said and stepped past him toward the door, skimming her fingers along his hand as she passed.

On the other side of the door, she grabbed the edge of it and leaned into it, looking back out into the hallway. Her face smoothed into an impassive mask, clear of anything that would help him understand if she found the revelations about his DNA too much now.

He stayed still until the door was shut, Zellendine on the other side.

Walking to his own quarters, he realized that he wasn't sure what he was going to tell Rullon about what had just happened, why it took so long for him to get back to bed. Was his dad worried? He wasn't sure, but he hoped not.

His own quarters were dimmed as he opened the door, two

of the bunks had their curtains closed, but the lights were still low.

Rullon sat at the table, his head on one hand, his eyes flying open as Troylus walked inside.

"Are you okay?" Rullon whispered, although with his voice it sounded more like a ball bearing was off in one of the central rotator's joints.

"Yeah, sorry. One of the fights was someone going after Zellendine and that was after Briar almost attacked her." Troylus dropped into the chair across from Rullon and rubbed his hands over his face.

His dad simply sat. Still and patient for news he knew Troylus was keeping, for news that Troylus still didn't understand how to say.

"Listen, I need to talk to you, but not tonight." Troylus gestured with his head toward the bunks and whoever was behind the curtains.

"Yep. I'm sacked. I'll see you in the morning," Rullon said, pushing on the table to get up, leaning closer to Troylus as he did.

"There's food in the server for you, one of the girls in the bunks went and got it for all of us, as a get to know you present." Rullon shook his head and went to lie down.

For him to so pointedly mention that they shared a space with girls made Troylus cough into a fist so he wouldn't burst out laughing. It wasn't that long ago, if he didn't count the years in stasis, that they shared their quarters with his sister. And they shared for years with his mom.

Why would girls being present make him so on guard?

A question for another day, Troylus decided, as he moved on to the server to see what kind of food these new people in his life liked to eat.

7

———

ZELLENDINE

She slept long past the chime calling for her to get up and get to the clinic. Some part of her brain was telling her to wake up, that it was time to start the day, but her body was beyond any level of exhaustion that she had known before.

By the time she was heading to the clinic to get the all-clear to start getting to work doing the checkups on others, the hallways were like navigating an asteroid belt. There were blocks in her way everywhere. They were human shaped and more than a little grumpy.

Some were carrying sacks of food for their servers while they waited for their turn in the clinic and their turn to get back to work.

When they were in classes as young children, they were told how many people were aboard, they were told how many different settlements there would be on the planet one day. Somehow, she was still unprepared for the level of crowding when everyone was awake.

The most frustrating part was how slow the throng moved. Why would more people in a space, everyone trying to get somewhere, mean that everything slowed? She shook her head as she finally walked into the clinic.

At least in here there were less people, only emergencies, those who needed medication for their time awake, and medics, were at the clinic for that day, and she was thanking the stars for that fact as she walked right back to find her dad.

He was tapping at a holo, the line between his brows showing, and his focus solely on the work in front of him.

"Stephen, could you give me the check?" she asked, coming up next to him and looking over his shoulder at the reports about Troylus.

The image on the holo made her suck in her breath.

Not only was there a whole extra part to Troylus's DNA, but there was a letter there, a representation of a new building block of DNA, entirely different from what she had ever seen before.

"How is that possible?" she asked, her voice barely audible.

"I don't know for sure, but look," he said, tapping on something that brought up a section of cells that looked suspiciously like it had been zapped with radiation.

"Does that mean what I think that means?"

"Radiation. In massive levels focused on one or two small sections. And by small, I mean only a handful of cells. Also, there is something here," he said, tapping another section and bringing up an image of Troylus's brain which had some activity in a section they never saw have activity.

"What in the stars does that mean?" she asked, looking at her dad, her mouth hanging open.

"I have no idea. I've never seen anything like it. It shouldn't even be possible. And I have his information. I even checked it against the scans I did when his eyes first started turning. It's part of his current file because it isn't supposed to change. What am I supposed to do with this? Save it in here? But then someone would wonder what the hell it even is." Stephen rubbed at the line between his brows, his mouth in a thin line.

"Hide it," she said, her voice too low for anyone else to hear.

"Excuse me?" he asked, opening his eyes and looking at her sidelong.

"Delete it. Pretend it was a misread. Nothing good can come of it." She was about to grab the holo from him and do it herself. After what she knew about the evil program in the mechanical wombs, she didn't trust that something wouldn't flag Troylus's test results and something wouldn't happen to him. She still didn't know if anyone on board knew and approved of what was happening in the wombs.

"Zellendine, if I do that, we will likely never be able to tell Troylus where this is coming from or how to stop it from turning more eyes silver around here." Stephen leaned in closer with every word, his eyes hard and his mouth not lessening in its rigid line.

"I don't care if every single one of us turns silver. Troylus will understand that it isn't worth the risk of him being found out." She grabbed the holo from her dad, her finger hovering over the image, waiting to tap out the command to erase all of it, taking a minute to hope Troylus would forgive her.

"Okay, wait," Stephen said, taking it back from her.

"No. We don't know what will happen if other people find out about this." She balled her hands into fists, trying not to snatch it back and run with it anywhere she could find on the ship and do what needed to be done.

"Listen, give me a couple days. I can keep this with me for a couple days, not let it out of my sight."

She opened her mouth to argue but he raised a palm and she closed it again, waiting for him to continue. Every minute he hung onto the information felt like an additional risk.

"No one wants more people on board, who for some strange

reason randomly want to attack certain people." Stephen remained motionless while she tried to suppress the urge to yell at him.

"Troylus got over the anger, and they will too. It's just a matter of time as they adjust to whatever is going on," she said, proud of herself that she didn't sound anywhere near as enraged as she felt.

"He wants answers to what's going on, and I would like the chance to find some for him."

Ouch. His words made her hands curl around her stomach as she bent forward enough to protect it. His words were like a physical blow. Troylus deserved answers. She had ignored his concerns about his eye before. She couldn't do that to him again — just ignore what he needed. She wouldn't do it.

"Fine, good, okay." She struggled to get in big enough breaths. Maybe she should stay away from Troylus. She clearly wasn't a good enough friend to think about what he wanted. The way back to her quarters loomed long in her mind at that moment, but she didn't want to be there anymore, so she turned to go.

"Zellendine, you still need your check for clearance," Stephen said, his hand touching the arm of her uniform enough for her to feel the fabric move, but not enough to press against her.

"Yeah." It was all she could think to say as she sat down and waited for him to examine her and run his scans.

It didn't take that long, he skipped part of it, but she barely noticed. Her mind was running over all the ways in which she had been hard on Troylus. All the ways in which she had not been as good to him as he was to her.

"So, I want to talk to you about the other thing you're concerned about," he said, as if it made sense.

"Huh?" she asked, shaking her head and focusing back on what he was saying.

"Your plan for once we touch down on the planet."

Oh. The plan to broadcast out to the other ships what the computer was doing with the wombs.

"Do you have some idea about that?" She wasn't sure why he was being cagier now when he was speaking more openly about Troylus just a little while ago.

"The room next to this one is full for right now, but if some others need to get clearance today, we can probably find time." Stephen turned to tap away at his hollow and raised his eyes to hers before he looked at the wall behind her.

Ah, so people could hear them now. Got it.

"Was there something you think we could do about my concerns?" she asked, her voice low and even, trying for bored if anyone did hear.

"I have an idea, but it will take me some more looking. If I find something, I'll let you know. It may be a way to do what you need to in regards to a solution," he said, managing a small smile and a wink.

He wasn't great at subterfuge. She repressed a smile, thinking about how glad she was that he excelled at finding a way to help people. Stephen was a lot of things, but one of them was a very good medic. Another was a damn good dad because she was snapped out of her pity party.

"I need to go find Troylus," she said, hopping up from the chair.

The smile on his face grew. She shook her head and smiled back.

8

TROYLUS

Even the orchard was too full of people. He couldn't get away from them. There was no specificity to them in his mind. He wanted to be away from practically everyone.

"Please let the planet have a lot of space for us," he said to the empty cryo bay as he stared out the window to the green, brown, and occasional blue of their new home as they got closer to it and he could start to see the colors as separate from each other.

The cryo bay was one of the only places on the ship that he could expect to remain alone. Supposedly the stasis crew had all been reassigned to something else after they made sure the tanks would remain in good working order for when they needed them again. He had no idea what crews they were assigned to. Maybe he was going to show up to the starwalker office the day after he got his clearance and there would be new people from stasis they would need to train. Maybe they were all in the service crew helping to make sure the ridiculous number of mouths were fed.

He decided he didn't really care. Even if there was another

starwalker, there would already be too many of them from all the shifts for him to learn their names. Unless they were going to be stuck on the planet together for a long time before everyone else came down, he didn't care to even try to get to know them all.

Zellendine had set off irrational rage last shift, now he wondered if the same thing was happening to him because of people in the crowds. Or maybe he was just a jerk who didn't like so many bodies and eyeballs around all the time.

A laugh escaped him, humorless, and with a melancholy to it he didn't like hearing.

"Screw it. Maybe I should just move in here." He leaned back against the stack of tanks behind him and wondered if it would be comfortable to actually sleep in the cryo tank or if he would miss his bed.

"If you do, can Stephen and I move in with you?" Zellendine asked, standing just inside the doorway, a small smile on her face.

"You don't like your new roommates?" he asked, leaning forward and putting his arms across his knees.

"No, I mean I don't know them at all. I'm sure they're fine. But I would feel safer and more... normal if I were in here rather than in my same quarters with strangers." She crossed the room and took a seat on the floor next to him, crossing her legs and looking out the window. Her face softened as she watched the last of the planet cross out of view of the window while the ship turned.

"Maybe I should talk to them and have them switch with us. I was serious when I suggested that." He didn't look at her while he offered again. He picked at a spot on the knee of his uniform.

"Troylus," she said, then she bit her lip and looked down at her lap.

Well, that reaction couldn't be good. Maybe he should have

just stayed quiet and pretended she wasn't going to turn him down and that she wasn't going to end up with Briar once he got over his irrational period.

"Listen, I don't even know what's going on right now. But I'm scared." Her voice cracked and he couldn't have looked away or stopped himself from reaching a hand out to her if he tried.

Forget trying to distance himself from her. If she was scared, he was going to be there to try and help.

"Zellendine, what can I do?" he asked, threading his fingers through hers.

She laughed the saddest laugh he had ever heard, shaking her head.

"Make it so that I can say, sure let's room up, like you're just my friend and it doesn't matter at all." Meeting his eyes, letting him see the tear running down one of her cheeks. Her bottom lip shook until she bit it.

"I..." he tried to answer, he tried to ask, he tried to say anything at all, but nothing came out past the first syllable.

Her lashes fluttered lower, her eyes falling from his face to the floor between them.

"Why does it matter, Zellendine?" he asked, his voice a whisper.

"Because..." She turned her face away from him and raised a shaky hand to her forehead. "Shit, I suck at this."

"This?" He leaned back, furrowing his brow. That almost sounded like it was some kind of mission, or some kind of trick she was playing on him. Was she that cruel? He didn't think so, but it was a strange thing to say and made his heart pound in his chest like it did right before he went out the airlock.

Zellendine swiped at her eyes and raised her face to him, her neck elongated so she was looking down her nose at him.

"Troylus—"

A massive crash and explosion sound from the hallway cut

her off, and sent her careening into his chest as he was knocked back toward the floor, barely catching himself with his hands so he didn't bounce his head off the hard metal. The door on the cryo bay started to close.

Just beyond the room, in the hall, screams rent the air before cutting off. Her body started to get dragged off him toward the too slow sliding door.

"No," Troylus screamed, flinging his hands out to grab Zellendine, but before he could, the blue light poured out of them and sealed off the opening to the hallway.

The air around them evened out, she stopped being sucked toward the door while it finished sealing itself off.

He forced himself to look at Zellendine, to keep his eyes locked on hers as she sat up and took deep breaths. It was the only way he could get the blue to stop. They didn't need it anymore, but part of him clearly didn't think it was safe still.

She put a hand on his leg, her breath hitching, and finally he could drop his hands to his sides and the blue light stopped.

"Does that mean what I think it does?" she asked, tilting her head toward the door, not letting go of him although her hand was shaking.

"I think so," he said. He didn't care if she were playing a trick on him, or if he would be the butt of a joke. He wrapped her in his arms and held her tight while tremors ran through her and her breathing hitched.

"We... we should... help." Her voice was stumbling and unsure, it only made him hold on tighter.

"Not yet." His voice sounded like he was growling, and maybe he was. It didn't matter if she ended up with Briar. He couldn't imagine ever not caring what happened to her.

9

ZELLENDINE

She clung to him, trying to calm her breathing and her heart. Finally, she thought she could speak without tripping over her own words.

"Troylus, we have to help," she said, not bothering to pull her face out of the crook of his neck. "We need to know what happened. How bad it is."

"I know." He didn't let go. He buried his face in her neck, his breath warm, sending chills down her back that calmed her.

"Come on," she said. "We need to check on our dads."

He let go of her then, scrambling to pull her to her feet. Once she was up, he wrapped her in a quick, tight hug before letting go and heading out the door on the other side of the room from whatever catastrophe had happened.

The hall was a melee, people were weaving in and out of each other trying to be the first to whatever destination they were headed toward.

"Shit," Troylus said, grabbing her hand and pulling her along, merciless in his march through everyone else.

More than one person was left swearing as they passed. She

wasn't sure if he was physically pushing people out of the way, but it wouldn't be a surprise to her if he did.

"I need to go that way," she said, tugging on his arm as they passed the branch to the clinic.

"But we'll have a better idea of what happened if we go to the starwalker office." He at least stopped pulling her along and stepped to the side of the hall, out of the direct way of traffic.

"Okay, you go, check with your crew, find Rullon. I'll go to the clinic and check on my dad. Whenever we get done, we'll meet up back at the..." She stopped and looked around as if the mass of bodies moving past them would help her come up with a good place to meet up.

"If you're not in the cryo bay, I'll find you at your quarters." He stared at her, and she couldn't help but think that this would be the perfect time for a hug. She wanted to reach out, but they both knew it wasn't wise, even if everyone was distracted.

He bit his lip and squeezed her hand before he turned and shoved his way through some other people that were just too damned slow for him.

She skirted along the wall, taking the turn toward the clinic she ran into someone, bouncing off their chest.

"Oh, Zellendine, have you seen Briar?" Journo asked, stepping back from her and putting a hand to his chest like she had scared him.

"No. I don't even know what's going on, I have to find my dad." Her voice was too high, she didn't want to explain anything to Journo, if he thought she was likely to know where Briar was, then he didn't know about their argument the day before. And the last thing she could hold in her brain was the possibility that Briar was in trouble. "Do you need me to help you find him?" She was only partially sure she wanted to offer it, but she did it anyway.

"Go to your dad, I'm sure we need medics right now. I'll get word to you when I know about Briar and the family." He nodded and headed off, disappearing among the many grey uniforms.

A part of her said to follow him, to find him, grab him, and go check on Briar, but the rest of her replayed his rage from the day before. She didn't trust that he wouldn't lash out at her violently. She definitely didn't think he would be happy to see her.

No, she decided, taking off down the hall toward the clinic, it would be better if she waited to find out from Journo. She would just have to pretend that no one she cared about was hurt by whatever had happened.

It would have been a lot easier if she could get her hands to stop shaking, and if she could just get through the damned crowd.

"Come on," she muttered, earning her a nod from the person next to her.

Finally, she put her arms together in front of her, pointing them forward like a needle and let them force the people away from the wall, giving her the narrow space needed to move.

She got to the clinic in time to see someone being carried in, their body hanging lifeless between the two people acting as transport, their arms hanging, flopping around with every hurried step of the people trying to get them help.

"What happened?" she said it out loud, although she wasn't really asking any of the panicked people milling through the space.

But her father answered her anyway.

He grabbed her into a hug before she knew what was happening.

"An explosion," he said into her ear before he pulled back and she realized he had a singed sleeve. In the center of the blackened area of fabric, some of the sleeve was burnt away entirely, the skin below it red and bubbled. His entire side was fire stained. Dark, angry splashes of black made him look like he was being grasped in the clutches of a monster made of ash.

"Dad, you're hurt," she grabbed his good arm and hauled him into an alcove where they kept the burn plant.

"No. I'm fine. Zellendine, listen," he said, yanking his arm out of her grasp.

"You're not fine. You're burnt." She snapped off a piece of the plant and smeared his burns with the juices from the inside, making him hiss in a breath.

"That's all we can do." He turned to head back to the rest of the clinic, but she grabbed him and slapped a bandage over the wound, making him yelp.

"Stop it. If you weren't such a stubborn ass, and held still, this wouldn't hurt. There are other medics, Dad." She snapped her jaw shut and fought the urge to swear at him more.

"I get it, but this is bad. And I'll live." He stared at her, his eyes wide, the fear in them plain, and she finally processed what the explosion meant, what his words meant about his own wounds.

"But some won't."

He nodded, his face softening into grief like she hadn't seen since her mother died.

Keep moving forward, she told herself and nodded. As much as she hated the Chapter's motto, now it was something she could use.

She followed her dad into a room where other medics were hooking someone up to a breathing machine and others were arguing over the best way to treat someone else.

Instead of joining that effort when there were already so many working on the person, she headed out to the main room, grabbed a holo along the way, and began the horrible task of triage.

Every time she looked at someone and made a choice about whether they could get back into the clinic right away or if they could afford to wait for a minute until someone was available, she was aware they might have internal injuries that even her holo scans couldn't see. With every second, and every decision, she was aware that she was taking the lives of the people in front of her into her hands.

The medic in her, her father's daughter, wanted to hold the people who were crying. Wanted to help each and every one of them right that second instead of doing the bare minimum to make them comfortable so she could help more people faster, and treat the ones that couldn't wait a second.

But she couldn't be that kind of medic today. Today she had to be the kind that barely saw her patients as people, they were just injuries to be categorized and prioritized. Today she had to be the perfect citizen of the Wheel and keep moving forward.

At least it kept her from thinking. Most of the time.

1 0

———

TROYLUS

IF ONE MORE FUCKING PERSON GOT IN HIS WAY, HE WAS LIKELY TO punch them in the face and just keep walking.

But, at last he could see the starwalker office ahead of him, and it seemed like he wasn't the only one who thought to come here.

He couldn't see Rullon, but he couldn't see through the crew members standing three deep clogging the doorway to the small office, so he wasn't panicked yet.

At the back of the pack, Parmita stalked back and forth, her arms wrapped around her abdomen, and her jaw tight like she was grinding her teeth.

"Princess, what's the story?" he asked, coming up beside her.

"Troylus," she said, her head popping up and a smile twitched on her lips before it fell off her face again. "Good to see you survived, Dumbass. Your dad is in there, they're trying to make sure the doors are all stable enough and nothing else is going to blow so we can all head out and start to fix this."

"I'm not sure I understand what exactly even happened." He

shook his head trying to believe that doors were the only thing saving the ship.

She didn't answer him, instead she turned to the group in front of the doorway, put two fingers between her lips and blew, hard. A whistle that made Troylus clap his hands over his ears made all the people standing around jump and cringe out of the way enough for him to dart into the crammed office.

"Oh, Troylus, thank the universe." Rullon said, leaning forward over the big console and taking a deep breath.

"What was that whistling for?" One of the people from another shift who sat at the console asked. He tapped on something and the holo in front of him changed.

"Ignore him. Did she tell you anything?" Maurice asked from where he was leaning up against the wall.

"No." Troylus would have said more to answer the question, but he was transfixed by the image on the holo. "Is that right now?"

Rullon looked up at him and nodded, his eyes pinched and his jowls more pronounced while he frowned.

"How in the hell did that happen?" The image of the ship on the holo looked like some massive space beast had formed from the depths of the universe and took a bite out of the ship. If their ship were an actual wheel, it wouldn't have rolled anywhere.

The people around him all turned to look at a woman who was sitting in one of the few chairs, staring at a wall, chewing in her fingernails and rocking back and forth in slow, small arcs.

Maurice nodded his head to a young woman with tiny braids in her hair that were tied back tight in a decidedly not regulation yellow sash that stood out even more against her deep brown skin and hair.

While she leaned down and whispered to the rocking woman, Troylus decided he needed to get to know anyone that was so comfortable flaunting the regulations. They would get along.

"One of them exploded. That's what happened," the rocking woman said around the fingernail she continued to chew.

"One of what?" he asked under his breath.

"Not what. Who." Her voice was eerie, made more so by the fact that she didn't seem to be seeing anything in front of her, and she sure wasn't talking to anyone in particular, it looked like she was just answering the questions to the galaxy.

"So, who exploded?" He couldn't believe he was asking that. People didn't explode.

"They were fighting. People were pulling them apart. I was just trying to get as far from another fight as I could. I can't have another meeting with leadership. They might make me stay onboard. I left them. I just left them. Next thing I know, I glanced back to see one of them explode in green light and I was flying. I don't know how I..." She didn't finish the sentence, but she didn't really have to. It was written all over her face as she squeezed her eyes shut and grimaced, rocking faster than before.

"No more of that. It's too much," the woman next to her said, putting a hand on her shoulder and turning silver eyes on Troylus.

His mouth dropped open and so did hers as they stared at each other.

"Did the person have..." he trailed off, letting the sentence hang, hoping she would know what he meant without outing his secret to the rest of the assembled crew.

She dropped her gaze and then lifted her eyes back to his, tears swam in them and he guessed.

Whoever the person was, they probably had the same eyes he and the new girl shared. They probably got in a fight for the same stupid reason so many fights were happening. But this time, the silver eyed person didn't manifest a power that remade a window. This time it killed a bunch of people and the bearer.

"Have what?" Maurice asked.

"Nothing. I don't know." He shook his head and focused back on the room and the problem they currently faced, but his idle thought to make a friend by talking to the woman turned into a burning need inside him, as strong as the need to breathe. He didn't need her as a friend. He needed to talk to her, to pick her brain about what, if anything, she knew about their eyes and what was happening to them.

"So, what are we waiting for exactly?" Troylus asked, pushing his way out of the office while Rullon swore and yelled his name.

"Princess? Can you help me?" he asked as he passed Parmita on the edge of the crowd.

"On it. Now I'm going to have to stop calling you names, huh?" she asked, darting over to his helmet.

"Nope. You can call me anything you want, as long as we get to work." He climbed into his suit, and with her help managed to get fully ready in record time.

By the time his helmet was on, the lady with the braids was suiting up too.

"Hey, help her out, then don't let anyone else out there, okay?" Troylus stared into Parmita's eyes as she furrowed her brow and bit her lip. He stared until she nodded and went to help the lady get suited up.

She probably wanted to go out there with them, but if Troylus and the other silver eyed person were going to be able to try and do anything beyond their normal level of work, they would need to be alone.

He could only hope it would be enough. And maybe, if he were careful, he could find out what she knew.

11

ZELLENDINE

They lost two more people. Two people who had been too close to a closing door. According to all of the witnesses, the doors only took seconds to slam shut, saying thousands of lives. There were even doors in the middle of the hallways that she hadn't known existed.

But in her mind, the time it took for the door to the cryo bay to shut, the agonizingly long time she remembered it being, as she was dragged off Troylus and air was sucked from her lungs, played over and over again.

At some point she was going to have to ask her dad how he had survived while being close enough to be burnt.

While she bandaged up an ankle that had been sprained in the scramble to get away from the site of the accident, she saw her dad sprint from one room to another, pulling on gloves as he went, and she knew it would be a long while before he took the time to explain anything.

"Zellendine," Journo said from behind her, his face tight and his hands wringing together in front of him as he stood at the threshold to the clinic.

"Hey, Journo, is everyone okay?" she asked, standing and turning to look at him, not bothering to say anything to the patient. Everyone seemed to understand the people darting in and out of the clinic with updates for their various connections.

"Physically? Yes. Emotionally... After you're finished here, I was wondering if you could come by and talk to Upton. He, um, well..." Journo turned to look at the wall and chew on his lower lip.

She gave him space. As much as she wanted him to spit it out, pressuring him wouldn't help right at that moment. Whatever was upsetting Upton, it upset his dad too. And there was more than enough to be traumatized by.

He shook his head and looked back at her, "Anyway, he can try and explain when you come to see him. Briar said he was going to be out this evening and all of tomorrow, so if you want to come by then."

Zellendine's cheeks heated up at the thought that Briar was still so angry with her he told his dad about it and made himself scarce so she could help his brother.

"Okay. No problem. I'll come by as soon as I can." She nodded and dropped back to her crouching position in front of her patient, hoping that Journo wouldn't ask her any questions about her and his son.

Peeking back, she watched as he left, and she could breathe again.

"There will be a lot of people who need help dealing with the trauma beyond just the physical wounds, won't there?" Chance said, sitting beside his mom as Zellendine wrapped her ankle for her.

He was almost old enough to start his apprenticeship, and she wondered if he was going to be one of the medics soon. If people were able to choose which crew they were assigned, she thought he likely would have picked to be in the clinic.

"Most likely, things like this…" She put the tape on the wrap so that it wouldn't unravel and grabbed the sealer to spray all over her work, protecting it until she used the counterseal spray in six weeks. "Well, when things like this happened before, people tended to take time to work through them. And that is fine. There is a lot we lost, and a lot that will never be the same, and a lot we still don't know. But, hopefully, with support from their friends and family, and some help if they need it, we will all be able to work our way through it."

She didn't realize what she said was wrong until she lifted her head after finishing with the spray sealant.

"Everyone needs to keep moving forward." Chance's eyes were wide as he stared at her.

Crap, there was never a great way to explain to some people about the ways in which they bent the rules to try and balance that motto with what they needed to do for people's mental health. And she sucked at trying.

"Of course. Some people just need a little extra help so they *can* move forward." He relaxed, so she thought she managed that time. After the trial at the last shift, she was going to have to be more careful.

They got their crutches and left the clinic. Before she was able to talk to her dad, she had to put it in the notes that she wasn't available for the mental health side of her job.

All their schedules were in their holos, so she tapped at hers and found the assignments calendar. How was she going to get out of the rotation, though? Especially since so many would need it.

Crying came from one of the rooms, and the low susurrations of her dad's voice, comforting the person, followed in its wake. He was so good at this, she was… not. If she could have gone back to the programmers of that first Chapter computer that chose their jobs for them, she would have punched them in the face.

Instead, she lied and tapped into the holo that all her time allotted for mental health services was already scheduled. Upton was going to get a very dedicated medic.

But for that minute, she had to check the vitals of the person who she saw carried in when she first got there.

The woman's partner was in the chair next to her bed, his head down and in his hands, he didn't lift it to look at her as she went about her business. He didn't seem to even be aware she was in there with them.

She couldn't help but wonder as she ran her scans and checked the tubes and wires the patient needed, what she would feel if she was in their position about the person that caused the tragedy.

For the silver-eyed, like Troylus and Briar, she hoped that everyone wouldn't label them all a threat. She hoped they would understand that the only times Troylus had used his power was to help her, except when they kissed, but she was pretty sure that was just it getting out of control.

The tube in her hand dropped back onto the bed, the rest of the line unchecked as she stumbled back under the weight of the possible breakthrough.

Lifting his head from the bed across from her, the man's face was stricken. Tears glistened in his eyes as he looked from her to the woman in the bed.

"Your partner's the same. Everything looks good. We'll keep on with this course of treatment, and I am hoping it will work for her." It was a lie and an empty platitude, but he relaxed and laid his head back down allowing Zellendine to breathe again.

She couldn't even think about the woman in the bed, or what she should be doing to help her anymore. She just turned and walked out of the room. If she were right, maybe they could do something about the powers erupting from people, about the rage, about all of the negative side effects of whatever was happening to the population of the Wheel.

TROYLUS

Outside the ship was new. The space around it so different from what he was used to it took his breath away. He couldn't see the wound in her side from just beyond the door lock, but what he could see was the bright light of the sun, large and glorious, filling his field of vision, bathing him in warmth that sunk deep into his bones.

He closed his eyes and the air moving through his lungs felt like it carried life giving joy.

"Troylus," Rullon's voice came over the comm, quavering and barely keeping it together.

"I'm okay. Trust me, this is best for now. We'll just take a look and assess and call for more help when we know what you should bring." He sighed and turned to grab hold of the ship. It didn't matter that he wanted to spend the whole month waiting to get to the planet, basking in the rays of the Grimm Star. He had a job to do.

"Who is we?" Rullon asked.

"Did you think I would let him come out here by himself?" The girl with the yellow in her hair said over the comm, slamming a hand onto the hold his was on and pulling herself up beside him.

"Imogene?" Another voice said over the comm. Troylus tried to match it to one of the faces crowded into the office and failed.

She cringed, shook her head and grabbed the next handhold.

"Right, so we'll just get to work, then." She pulled herself along the same way he always did, without using the boosts of air, just hand over hand while her tether spooled out behind her.

He hurried to catch up to her, waving a hand once he did until she turned toward him.

With exaggerated movements, he turned off his comm and she followed suit.

"If we leave them off for long, they'll notice and break through," she said.

"Maybe you should go to the cryo bay just the other side of the damage later, just to make sure the door is holding. Can't be too careful," he said, and tapped his comms back on.

She nodded and followed his lead.

Even if he wasn't going to get to talk to her until later, and even if they weren't able to get much done for repairs, the trip into the stars was already worth it by her agreeing to talk to him. Maybe he would be able to get Zellendine in on the conversation too.

Ahead of him she paused, hanging onto the handhold, not a bit of her moving.

Reaching her position, he tried to steel himself, told his heart to look at everything as just another broken part that needed fixing. This was a mechanical problem, and they were uniquely prepared to remake the world in front of them, it would be fine.

But nothing could have stopped his soul from aching at the damage he saw, nothing could have made him ready to see bodies, and parts of bodies, still trapped by wreckage that used to be a hallway.

"No," Imogene whispered, their comms making her low voice carry with all the weight of the universe to him and those listening inside.

"Imogene? What do you see? Can we fix it?" Rullon asked, his voice matching hers in his low tone and careful enunciation. As if they were both worried that if they said more or weren't careful in their language it could all be worse.

"Rullon, this is bad, but we need to do more checking to give you an idea," Troylus said, his voice was too loud. He winced, but he had to focus and get to work because he didn't want to be left crying inside his helmet. Moving past her, although he didn't want to, he took his tether and used it to collect the bodies of those he thought the families would want to see. The rest he let go into the stars, including the pieces that he didn't want to think about.

She trailed behind him doing the same, until they were left with mangled and torn metal and ship interior.

One of the floorboards broke off as he touched it and floated away.

He tapped his comm again to turn it off and waited until she did the same.

"Are you ready? Can you do this?" If he felt his soul was wounded by the scene before, the nerves while he waited on her answer were shredding his stomach.

"Yes. I…" She turned to look out at the planet, still so far away. "I haven't fixed anything before, but I think it's our best chance."

"Last shift I remade a window." It was his turn to look at the planet and hope they would make it, that their abilities would see them to it instead of destroying them at the door.

"Really?" Her eyes were huge behind her helmet and he almost laughed, but it died an early death in his throat.

"Before they get worried, let's try this."

Together they turned back to the gaping maw of the terrible scar on the ship.

He tried to find the place inside his mind and heart that he unlocked when the window was broken, holding his hands out in front of himself.

And nothing. No blue light, just regular Troylus, looking more than regular levels of foolish.

"Uh, I don't know how to call on it," he said, looking at his hands, although he knew they didn't hold any secrets.

"And I was hoping to watch you fix it. I thought you knew," she said, her shoulders slumping.

"No. I just know that if we can make this work, we could fix the hole." He put a hand to his helmet, which only made him more frustrated that he couldn't rub the back of his neck or push hair his mind still expected to be too long out of his eyes.

Zellendine was so close to death the times he had called on it before...

He looked back at the bodies of those who weren't lucky enough to be in the cryo bay with them. Instead of turning away from the horrifying reality of their deaths, the fear that must have flood them in their last seconds, he allowed himself to imagine that they were all Zellendine. That he was not able to save her, and he was picking up the pieces of her shattered remains after the fact.

Blue light poured out of him and he focused on the ship, to make it safe again.

"It's working. How?" Imogene yelled, although she didn't have to, she was right next to him and their helmets were always connected via comm even when they weren't linked to the office.

Troylus's breath was ragged as he let go of the blue light and had to brace himself on her arm, bent forward while sweat poured down his back.

"Somehow..." he started, taking long breaths before he finished, "it's connected to thinking about someone I love getting hurt."

Metal was still mangled and malformed in front of them. He had made it better, but it was still destroyed. Every muscle in his body ached, and he wasn't sure he had the ability to fix it entirely.

"Okay," she said. "I shouldn't put it all the way back together, but to something that they can finish for us."

Imogene nodded, lifted her hands out in front of her and held her body as rigid as the floorboard that had floated past their heads.

Yellow light, shimmering like it was a solar flare she could hold in her hand, flowed out of her, wrapping around pieces and bending them effortlessly back into sheets.

When she was done, she collapsed into his side and in front of them the ship looked like the explosion had blown out in such a way that all the metal was just peeled back, exposing a badly damaged interior.

He tapped his comms back on and did the same for her.

"Troylus? Uh..." Rullon said, and he cringed at what their little reconstruction project had looked like to the ship's scanners.

"All kinds of things are damaged out here." Troylus set Imogene against the handhold and grabbed on himself. "Censors are probably destroyed, shields are gone, and we can walk through the hole to the interior. But we, um..." He paused to look at the gruesome tail they had created for themselves of the bodies.

"Um, what?"

"We're bringing in some of the fallen, so their families can say goodbye." Troylus heard the intake of breath on the other end and the low rumble of too many voices saying too many things that followed.

But Imogene nodded her head, and he took it as a sign that they needed to get back inside the ship. The others could do the rest of the work. Hopefully his offhand comment about the censors and the state of the ship's wound would cover for them.

They had done enough, and he had a lot of questions for Imogene.

13

ZELLENDINE

She didn't want to knock on the door. People moved past her, unaware that she was frozen in place. But she had been to the orchard and the cryo bay. Troylus wasn't in either. She had to keep moving or the need to tell him what she had figured out would drive her to distraction.

Briar's door, the one she had been to a thousand times, dropping him off and picking him up, had never scared her before. He wasn't even in there. She knew that. Journo had assured her. But it felt wrong for her to walk into his space, and it wasn't just because of the protocols.

In an emergency, sure, she would be forgiven for breaching their privacy by going in, but would she ever feel right breaching Briar's boundaries when she knew he was furious with her?

Part of her wanted to believe that he would eventually get over his issues with her like Troylus had, but part of her worried he wouldn't. And every last bit of her thought that this little intrusion, no matter that it was for the right reasons, would make any reconciliation less likely.

Her hand shook as she raised it and left it hanging in the air an inch from the door.

Someone in the crowd passing through the hall bumped into her so she stumbled into the door, knocking on it with more than just her knuckles.

There was barely time to stand up straight before it swung open to silver eyes.

Zellendine swallowed and stepped back, colliding with someone else, reminding her she couldn't just turn around and head to her quarters.

"I'm leaving," Briar shouted over his shoulder into the room and shoved her out of the way, barreling into the traffic of bodies, leaving swearing people marking his passage.

A sighing Journo appeared in the doorway, shaking his head.

"Come in, please." He held the door open for her and she tucked her holo against her chest, holding onto the edges too tight, to keep her hands from shaking as she walked in.

She wasn't sure how to feel about Briar and the way he was acting, but she couldn't think about it at that moment. She had a job to do. And it was more important than Briar.

"Hi, Zellendine," Upton mumbled from a spot on a bed, ensconced in blankets so only his little face showed.

"Buddy, are you cold?" she asked, moving to the side of the bunk to crouch down by him.

"Yes. I can't get warm anymore." He shivered.

For a moment she could only see the little boy who was trapped inside his dreams last shift. She could only see the worry and the fear everyone had on his behalf and on behalf of the other sleepers hanging around him like a miasma.

Zellendine forced a smile onto her face and lifted her holo. Upton was alive and she was going to treat him like he was.

"Do you mind if I run a few scans. I'll see if there is a way to get you feeling warm again." She tapped away at her holo until it showed the beginning of the scans she wanted to run and then turned it so Upton could watch as information poured into it and changed the figures.

"I know it's just a computer, but it's like art too," he said, his voice low and wistful.

For a small boy who was usually so full of energy, he sounded like he was as old as the stars. It sent a shiver up her spine as she glanced at Journo and his partner, standing to the side.

They held hands, their grips tight on each other.

"Okay, Upton, do you want to tell me about what's been bothering you?" she asked, "Is it the accident that happened? Your dads have been worried for you."

"It's more than the accident. The accident just says I'm right." He tucked his chin inside the edge of the blanket and cast his eyes down to his lap.

"Right about what?" Asking the question sent a chill down her spine, although she couldn't have said why. When he lifted his eyes to hers, a tiny shard of silver glinted in one of his irises. A shiver ran down her back and the hairs on her arms stood on end.

"People are going to die. You can't be one of us. It doesn't want you here." His voice was a whisper, dark and deeper than it should have been. His focus wasn't on her face, but somewhere beyond her that she couldn't see.

"What doesn't want me here?" Her throat was dry, and her hushed words came out harsh and scratchy.

"I..." He shook his head and looked at her, instead of through her, his lower lip trembling, "I don't know, Zellendine. I don't know."

A tear ran down his cheek and she wanted to reach out to comfort him, protocols or not, but she couldn't force herself to move.

"O-" she choked on the word and had to cough into her hand before she tried again. "Okay. How about we go over these scans and make a schedule for us to talk about it some more. Would that be okay with you?"

He took a deep breath, a wavering smile forming on his face as he relaxed back into the pillows behind him and nodded.

"So," she looked down at her holo, almost dropping it. The readings mapped the last few minutes of his vital statistics. Whatever just happened, it wasn't a regular discussion.

Tapping at her holo, Zellendine tried to examine all the information. It was too much for her to process, it didn't make sense. It would take her days to even try and make sense of it.

Maybe she could get Stephen to look through it with her before she saw Upton again. Maybe he would be able to tell her what it all meant.

No scans she had ever seen looked like Upton's. No one's ever should have looked like his did.

Journo cleared his throat, and his partner was leaning toward her, his mouth open and his eyes wide while a vein pounded so hard in his neck, she could see it from five feet away.

Looking from them to her tiny patient, she realized she had been silent for too long while she examined all the information.

"Well, I know why you can't get warm," she said, and they all relaxed.

But she didn't know why his temperature was fluctuating so wildly, or why the spikes of his temperature were above what would give most people a seizure.

14

TROYLUS

IN FRONT OF HIM, THE LAST OF THE AIRLOCK DOORS OPENED.
Imogene stepped across the threshold and motioned for the others to come and help.

Parmita disconnected both of them from their tethers. He couldn't bring himself to look back at the grisly work he left to the others.

"What the fuck, Troylus? I..." Parmita said, her voice trailing off as she glanced over his shoulder and shuddered.

"Yeah." He couldn't bring himself to say much more. She wasn't asking why he and Imogene had brought them inside. At least he didn't think so. Parmita was probably just as worried and confused as everyone else about why it had happened in the first place.

She helped them climb out of their suits and put them away for them.

Rullon popped his head out of the office as Troylus passed by and placed a hand on his son's arm.

Troylus nodded to his dad and kept walking. He didn't want

to be questioned, he didn't want to try and explain to Rullon or anyone else. He didn't want to talk at all about the walk.

He made his way down the hall from the office and looked back long enough to spot Imogene, with her bright yellow hair tie, making her way through the thickening crowd in the hall.

Every step beyond the starwalker office meant more people he had to navigate through. Why didn't the Chapter plan for more room when everyone was awake?

He wanted to scream at all of them. He just wanted to be able to walk without running into someone.

No matter that he hated the protocols, every time he bumped into a body it felt weird. The only people he was comfortable touching were his crew, his family, Briar, and Zellendine. That list didn't even include most of the people on his shift, let alone all the people moving past him whose names he didn't know.

Finally, he reached the cryo bay, but it was no longer a refuge.

Stopped in his tracks, one foot in front of the other, Troylus stared open mouthed at the people scattered through the room.

There were two blankets on the floor with small groups sitting on them talking in low tones. By the tanks, three couples leaned against the stacks and each other, looking out the window.

"Where did they all come from?" he asked under his breath to no one. Why weren't they all in their own cryo bays? Why were they invading this one?

"I guess this conversation will have to be a little different than I was expecting," Imogene said, coming to stand at his side before she walked into the bay.

"Do none of them realize that the only thing between them and space is a damn door?" he asked, shaking his head and following her.

"You're here," she said over her shoulder as she turned the corner between two stacks.

"Not the same." He wanted to roll his eyes. She knew it wasn't the same for them as it was for this collection of strangers.

Imogene turned and sat, leaning against the wall, and looking up at him with her silver eyes that matched his.

Troylus took a seat beside her, pulling his knees up so he could lean his arms against them while he looked out the window.

"How did you realize?" He wasn't sure how else he was supposed to ask the questions he needed to, so he just left out any specific mentions of their lights.

"Parts of it are hard to explain. I woke up my last shift with my eyes like this, and I was pissed off with a couple people on my shift. People I liked who had done nothing negative to earn my anger, so I knew something was really wrong with me." She picked at one of her cuticles and he realized it probably wasn't fair for him to expect her to tell him everything when he had not confided anything in her.

So he told her the story of that first time his ability showed up. She had broken protocol, so he assumed she wouldn't panic about Zellendine and him looking back, and as much as he assumed she knew turning him in to leadership would risk her own secret getting out, he couldn't bring himself to tell her everything.

"An anomaly?" She was staring at the side of his face and it made him want to hide, but he didn't. He nodded instead.

"Mine manifested when I was on a walk too, but it wasn't because of an anomaly." She took a deep breath and focused back on the space beyond the window. "My tether broke."

He sucked in a breath, the air hissing through his teeth. It was one of his greatest nightmares.

"I didn't have the time or the clarity to use the air to propel me. I just reached out and the yellow pulled me to a handhold."

"When we were out there you seemed to know exactly how to use it, how did you do that?" His voice was barely audible and his eyes darted around taking stock of how far away people in the room were and how likely they were to hear him. Even if people didn't understand what they were talking about, he didn't want anyone to form any questions.

"After the first time I used it on a walk, I tried to do it again. I worked on it when I was out there by myself, or when I was on the other side of the ship from my crew member. It took a while for me to figure out that I could control not only when it came out of me, but what I did with it."

Troylus snapped his head to the side to look at her, his mouth working, but no words coming out.

Somehow it had never occurred to him that he could do all of that with his ability. There had to be some kind of limit on what they could do, but how they would gain the space to find out what it was, he couldn't imagine.

"Have you not practiced?" She asked, turning to face him.

"I... No. I haven't."

"But you seemed to know what you were doing out there."

Furrowing his brow and turning away from her again he thought about it, about whether that was actually true.

"You know, before we went, I knew we could do it. Because of the first time, I knew that fixing was possible. But I wasn't so sure I could make it happen. Until I thought about the times it had." He rubbed his hands over his face, just talking about it, the emotions he had to call on, gave him a fresh wave of exhaustion.

"That was one of the first lessons I learned too. It's somehow connected to our emotions. I think it's why we all have the rage. Not that I've figured out why it's directed at the people it is, but it makes sense that whatever caused this also caused us a way to be forced to realize we had it."

She was just musing, looking out the window and paying no attention to him next to her or even the fact they weren't alone. It was clear she was deep inside her own head.

He was lost inside his own mind too. For him, the focus wasn't on what could have caused their abilities, or even on the fact that he was right about the emotional connection to it.

No, his focus was entirely on the people who were the targets for the rage. Maybe Imogene could be satisfied with having no answers as to why certain people were targeted, but she didn't have as strong a connection to the person that had pissed her off the most.

Figuring that part out was probably going to be up to him and Zellendine. Because with Briar's anger focused at her too, she was clearly in danger from any of the people who looked like he did. And now he knew for sure that they were all as powerful as he was.

15

ZELLENDINE

She did all the things she knew to do, the medications, and the instructions on a wash, but there were no good answers for Upton or his dads. All she could really offer them was to offer calm that masked her desperate attempt not to panic so she didn't lead them to panic too.

Maybe her dad would have an answer.

Her mind kept returning to that improbable hope because he always had before. And when he didn't, he at least had a way to make you feel like there was one and he would keep looking until he found it.

Zellendine didn't have that ability, especially because she suspected she knew what the cause of Upton's strange symptoms were. Or at least she thought they were related, even if his eyes weren't completely overtaken by silver.

There was just no way she could see that the two were disconnected entirely.

All the people in the halls made her walk slow and allowed her mind to wander through the charts she had seen — the charts of Upton and Troylus.

Part of her wanted to find Troylus and tell him all the things she had discovered, or at least all the things she thought she might find at the end of her current search.

More important than that conversation, she needed to track down her dad and get him to spend some time helping her find answers. Stephen had Troylus's chart anyway.

He said he was going to study it more. Maybe he had been able to come up with something.

A stray thought popped into her mind: What if they could reverse the changes? Would she suggest they do that? Would Troylus want that?

The thought of deciding for someone made her cringe. It was a little too close to the decisions the Chapter computers made for them all.

But for some people, Upton included, how could they as medics endorse something that seemed to be hurting the person who was going through it? Should she look at it like a surgery? That sometimes to do the most good at the end required a step through harm?

Rubbing her eyes, she rounded the corner to the clinic, still packed full of people after the disaster.

Whatever solace she sought in going to her father was lost in the pain and the fear of the people around her. She was too wrung out to be there. She needed to go, anywhere but there.

But she had to find her dad first.

Patients and medics, their friends and family, waited in the rooms. But none of them were her father.

Maybe he had to make a report to leadership.

For most of her life his duty as part of leadership didn't bother her, but just the thought of him making a report to them made her stomach flip and her throat run dry.

Taking a deep breath, she forced herself to remain calm because she could trust her dad.

Zellendine made her way back out of the clinic and into the masses in the hall.

Leadership wasn't in session when she stopped by the gathering room. Instead, there were tons of people weeping, some of them in desperate sobs that clawed and scratched at her soul.

Bodies were everywhere, under sheets and motionless.

Even after the terror and the agony of the people she saw in the clinic, after the triage and the worry, she was not fully prepared for the level of devastation surrounding her in the gathering room.

Zellendine scanned the faces of the mourners, their eyes red, their cheeks tear streaked, and those that looked like they were in shock. She took them all in, not that she wanted to, but it would have been just like her dad to be there and offering what he could.

Instead, she saw other medics weaving through the people. A still no sign of him.

Where was he?

None of it made sense to her as she wandered away from the gathering room. He wasn't going to just run off when there was so much work to be done that he was able to accomplish. That wasn't like him.

The orchard was full, but neither he nor Troylus were there. The cryo bay was also filled, but empty of the people she was looking for.

How was she supposed to find him in the throngs of people and the pandemonium of the disaster's aftermath?

16

TROYLUS

HE WANDERED, AIMLESSLY, ALLOWING HIMSELF TO BE SWEPT along, for hours. He roamed the halls temporarily not angry with the crowds. At least they were heading somewhere and gave him a direction.

There was too much in his head, too many things to think about.

Mid step he stumbled, part of him wondering why and the other scanning the people in front of him.

Did he see something? If he did, what?

Under his feet, the ship lurched, the same engine acting up kind of movement that plagued him all last shift but that the engine crew didn't seem to notice.

The engine rooms weren't that far from where he was. So he made the turn their way.

He wasn't doing anything important anyway, he might as well actually ask the engine crew what was going on instead of just looking in at them and making an assumption.

Ahead a ways in the hall, turning toward a door before the

engine room, one he was sure he had never seen open before, was Zellendine.

Her blonde hair wasn't why he knew it was her. Nor was it the uniform she wore that looked the exact same from behind as everyone else on board. No. And it wasn't a specific thing about her walk. He just knew.

She paused. More than that. It looked like someone had tapped a holo and turned her off. She was frozen, staring into the dark of the other side of the open door.

And then her freeze stopped.

Zellendine screamed.

Her hands flew to her mouth, trembling while her voice was a steady wail.

People in the hall tripped over each other trying to back away from her like whatever tragedy she saw would leap across the space between them through the power of her voice.

Troylus shoved and yelled, throwing people out of his way, heedless of what happened to them.

Zellendine kept screaming.

17

ZELLENDINE

"No!" It was all that would come out of her mouth, endless shrieking and the word "no," over and over.

There was no way it was true. Her brain couldn't wrap itself around the horror of it, it couldn't accept the reality. Because in no universe did it make sense.

Arms wrapped around her as her legs gave out.

Her screaming didn't stop.

All the muscles in her body lost their ability to work, turning to liquid. Her lungs and her vocal cords took up all her strength, trying to force the universe to hear her anguish.

"Oh, stars, Stephen," Troylus said above her, his voice quaking.

She didn't hear his voice so much as feel his words move through her as her eyes remained unblinking on the charred body of her father. Her screams reverberated off the walls.

"Come on, Zellendine. Step away. Shhh." He tried to pull her away from the remains, but she replanted her numb legs, still screaming, "no."

Under no circumstances was she going to be taken away

from this. She had to see it, to commit all the details to memory because she knew she needed to revisit it all later. She couldn't do it yet, but she needed to eventually. She needed to know what happened.

"No," she screamed again, her voice cracking as she threw herself on the floor near his body, only stopped from careening into him by Troylus grabbing for her.

Near Stephen's outstretched hand, still wrapped in the bandage Zellendine had made him put on, his holo sat on the floor. It was dark and a sob broke through her screams. Was this last, small token of him broken?

Troylus tried to pull her to her feet. She smacked him, shoving him away from her.

She snatched the holo and clutched it to her chest, allowing herself to finally be drawn away from the remains of her father.

His eyes were open, staring into nothing, taking in nothing.

One whole side of his torso, including his arm and up part of his neck, was a scorched, twisted mockery of flesh. His uniform, where it wasn't gone completely on that side, was indistinguishable from the parts of his skin and muscle that had been reduced to ash. There was no smell that normally accompanied burned human, and the lines between where he was burned and where he was whole were so clear it looked like they didn't belong to the same body.

When the accident happened, his uniform was singed and his burns faded in and out across his skin. This was the difference between a star and an asteroid.

It couldn't be real.

It didn't make sense.

It would never, even if she came to know how and why it happened, ever make sense.

Just like Stephen, her father, the only family she had left, would never be with her again.

Zellendine's voice gave out. It broke down into sobs, silent and wrenching, they felt as if they would turn her inside out.

"Shhh," Troylus whispered into her ear, arms holding her tight.

But he didn't need to shush her anymore, she had nothing more to say.

18

TROYLUS

Zellendine was inconsolable. He was lost, scrambling in his mind for the right words, any words to say to help, to make it better. Even if it could only help a fraction, he wanted to be able to give her that. But there were no words for this. There was no way to make this better.

He didn't want to look at Stephen like that. The man helped everyone, devoted his life, far beyond even most medics, to helping everyone on board. He didn't deserve whatever had caused the damage Troylus saw all over his body.

After the people he had collected on his walk, he never expected to see death again so soon. Least of all in the form of this man. Zellendine shuddered in his arms and he renewed his grip on her, biting his lip and fighting back his own tears.

People in the hall milled about, most of them keeping a respectful distance, and some even stopped others from breaching the small circle he and Zellendine took up in the middle of the floor. He wanted to thank them, but she needed his attention. Those people didn't.

Some piece of his brain knew leadership, or their representatives, would be along eventually and it made him keep looking toward the main corridor. But all he could think about clearly was what he needed to do for Zellendine now that her father was dead.

Could he trust that her roommates would treat her with the care she deserved after this? He wasn't sure.

Poor Zellendine needed people to make sure she would eat, to keep an eye on her. No one deserved to find their dad this way.

Finding someone dead was one thing, but to see them after they had been killed?

He shook his head against the top of her hair where she was tucked under his chin and against his chest.

Stephen's burned arm and hand were curled up in an unnatural, tight, and contorted way in front of him, but that lonely whole hand reaching out to nothing... It was haunting and Troylus wondered if Zellendine was going to see it in her sleep.

In a dark corner of his mind, he wondered if they would be able to measure the same kind of radiation that Stephen had found evidence of in Troylus's scans.

The crowd shifted and moved, the general noise level rising. Zellendine seemed unaware of the activity starting around them.

Members of leadership from another shift, Troylus could tell by the way people around them acted, arrived with helpers in tow.

None of them were members of their same shift, but every single one of them stopped and had to take a moment to compose themselves before they tried to move Stephen's body. One even turned back to face the crowd, closing their eyes, and didn't turn back.

As soon as the first person touched Stephen though, the

hush that everyone was operating in was shattered by Zellendine's scream.

She thrashed in Troylus's arms, trying to fling herself in the direction of her father's body.

"You should get her to her quarters, she doesn't need to see this." One of the leadership team crossed to Zellendine and crouched down, blocking her view to the body. Their eyes were soft and their mouth in a sad smile. "I promise, we will be as careful and respectful as possible. He was a wonderful man, and so proud of you."

Zellendine didn't stop thrashing, she only grew more frantic in her efforts.

The leader closed their eyes, squeezing them shut as if they were in pain themselves, then made eye contact with Troylus and nodded before they stood back up and headed to their duty.

He took it as a signal that his duty was to find a way to get Zellendine away from that scene.

"I'm going to pick you up and carry you to your quarters," he said, hoping she would forgive him for doing it.

She wailed and threw her head back, howling toward the ceiling as Troylus lifted her in his arms and moved toward the crowd who parted in silence and averted their eyes.

Grief, especially the way Zellendine was showing it, wasn't something that should have had protocol attached to it, but he couldn't help thinking the people in the hall were uncomfortable around someone being so open.

But to him, she was making the same sounds and the same moves he wanted to when his mother died. He envied her bravery. As a child, all he allowed himself to do was cry, silent, wracking sobs that screamed to the universe in salt what he wouldn't allow his voice to.

He hoped she got a better response than he had back then.

Carrying her around the last bend to exit the hall with her

father in it was like he put a shield over the action center of her brain. She stopped thrashing and turned into a limp siren, the only thing moving her vocal cords.

No matter how limp she was, her grip on Stephen's holo never lessened.

19

ZELLENDINE

She was lost in a black hole, spinning and aimless. Alone, floating and falling forever, but she had her father's holo. It was the only thing that could save her. Without it, she would never find her way out of the dark.

Her hands and arms ached with the effort to keep the holo close to her, with the effort to not allow it to fly off into the darkness.

And she couldn't stop the high pitched, piercing cry that flowed in waves past her as she fell.

2 0

TROYLUS

By the time they reached the hall where her quarters were, his arms felt like they were going to fall off his body, but there was no fucking way he was going to drop her.

Just beyond her door, Briar stood in the corridor, his mouth hanging open as his eyes narrowed and his hands balled into fists at his sides.

"Hey, did you hear?" Troylus called out to him, but Briar didn't hang around to answer the question, or even acknowledge he heard it.

Instead, Briar turned on his heel and stormed through the hall, people moved aside by force instead of moving willingly and respectfully like they were for Troylus with the still screaming Zellendine in his arms.

Knocking on the door to her quarters, in his mind he begged the stars for someone to be on the other side.

The door opened and Rullon reached out to scoop her out of Troylus's grasp.

Zellendine began to thrash again, and Troylus stumbled, almost dropping her after making it so far with no problem.

With Rullon's help, he moved her to one of the beds, the largest one, and folded her into the blankets.

She buried her face in the pillow, her body stilled, and her screams stopped. The only sound she made was the quiet anguish of tears that he was sure she thought would never stop.

He crouched down beside her, putting a weak and shaking hand to her shoulder, and he tucked the blankets just a bit tighter.

No matter how much he wanted to climb in beside her and hold her, tell her everything would be alright, he knew he couldn't.

Because making that promise when he wasn't sure if it was a lie seemed cruel.

Rullon shook his head and moved to the table, taking a seat and putting his head in his hands.

"How are you here?" Troylus asked, collapsing into the seat across from him and putting his head down on the cool surface.

"Leadership sent a runner, they told me we needed to move in here because they wanted her to have someone," Rullon said, shaking his head again, his jowls more pronounced than Troylus had ever seen them.

Troylus lifted his head and slumped back in the chair, wishing he had the strength to get up so he could hug Rullon.

"Thank you, Dad."

Rullon snapped his head up and looked into Troylus's eyes, nodding once.

"We should get some food into you. You must need it after that." He turned and looked at where Zellendine laid in the bed, her shoulders shaking as she sobbed. "She needs some food too."

She did. Troylus knew that, but he bit his lip wondering when the next time would be that she would actually be willing to get anything down.

"I'll try to get her to eat something," he mumbled, hoping any attempt he made wouldn't just make her worse.

He didn't know how to do right by her, how to navigate through this with her. All he could do was try, and hope he didn't screw up so badly he made anything harder for her.

"Leadership didn't tell me, what happened to..." Rullon trailed off and squinted his eyes to Zellendine, like he was trying to think of a good way to say 'Stephen' without actually saying his name.

Troylus coughed, drawing his dad's eyes and he glanced at the wet room, getting up on shaking legs that wanted to cramp halfway up, and heading in that direction.

Rullon followed him into the wet room and he whispered what little they knew for sure into his dad's ear.

After he was done, Rullon stood still with his eyes squeezed shut as a tear escaped anyway and trickled down his cheek.

For some reason, Troylus had forgotten that his father and Stephen had known each other for as long as he had known her, and likely they shared stories he had no idea had ever happened. He put a hand on his dad's shoulder and squeezed as much as his worn out hands could.

"Stephen would take care of you and Indigo," Rullon said, opening his eyes and nodding. "We're going to take care of Zellendine."

He patted Troylus on the shoulder and left the wet room. Giving Troylus the space he needed to lean against the wall and make wish after wish, to every star he had ever seen and all the ones he hadn't, that his dad would make it.

Whatever was happening, the rising threat of people who couldn't control themselves, the people who might be targeted by a silver that he couldn't warn, the whole population that deserved to be informed of so much and couldn't be allowed to know a thing because the reprisal from leadership would be swift, he just wanted the small group he cared about so much he wasn't sure he could make it without them, to live.

He walked out of the wet room and Rullon set plates down on the table.

"There's more for Zellendine, but I want you to eat something. It will give her a little more time." Rullon sat and started eating.

For Troylus, the food was a nice gesture and what he needed, but what he really wanted was to be able to make the kind of treats his mother knew. Rullon may have been good with a service, but his mom knew how to come up with fantastically sweet and delicious small treats. Not meals, really, just the best tiny bites he had ever eaten.

Looking over at Zellendine, he thought that those would have been more welcome to her at that moment too.

"Rullon," Troylus said, after he ate his last bite of food and his dad had just put his last bite in his mouth. Rullon nodded as he chewed, urging him to continue.

"It's time. I said I would tell you when I knew how to. I'm still trying to figure out the right words to use, but you need to know. Even if I stumble through it all."

His dad leaned back in his chair.

"You're right. Because I have a feeling all of this is connected, all the things happening right now." He raised his eyebrows at Troylus who could only nod.

He started his story from the moment he woke up furious with Zellendine last shift, even though he repeated some things, to where he was sitting in her quarters, willing to do almost anything for her.

When he was done talking, he was exhausted. More than just his body, his whole soul and mind were ready to pass out.

But there were more important things that night than sleep. He could sleep after he was done.

Rullon stared at the table in front of him, his mouth set in a grim line.

"I have to say, I knew something was going on, but whatever I had conjured up in my head, it wasn't this." Rullon smiled, and raised his eyebrows while he stifled a laugh, glancing towards the bed.

"You—" Troylus almost choked on his words, "You're laughing?"

"No. But, come on. This explanation is kind of funny."

Troylus just stared at him, his mouth hanging open.

"Okay, fine. Yes, it sounds bizarre. But you are not a liar, and I'm still going to be your dad, even if I don't have some special light ability to fix things." He shook his head, grabbing a smaller amount of food from the service, gesturing with his head toward the bunks, holding the food out to Troylus.

He smiled at his dad, shook his head, and brought the food to Zellendine.

She was asleep. Instead of waking her up, instead of worrying about one skipped meal when she probably needed the sleep more, he set the food down beside the bed and laid down next to her, curling around her on top of the covers.

"People are still here for you, Zellendine. I'm still here, and so is Rullon. We'll be here for anything you need. I'm so sorry." His voice was hushed as he spoke to the back of her head and hoped that the knowledge sunk into her sleeping mind so at least she would feel a tiny bit less alone when she woke up.

21

ZELLENDINE

WARM. SHE WAS SO WARM. FOR A MINUTE SHE THOUGHT HER mother was still alive and she was wrapped in her arms.

It happened from time to time. Had since her mother passed, but she must have needed a lot of support if her dad was holding her gently, wrapped around her, with an arm draped over her side.

But... Her dad was dead too.

Everything poured back through her mind, the horror and the agony of the day before. She sucked in a breath, and it exploded from her in a chest caving sob as she threw the arm of whoever it was off her and jumped from the bed.

"Zellendine? It's okay," Troylus said, popping up in the bed and rubbing his eyes.

"Okay?" Her voice cracked, and she would have been screaming at him, but a hoarse scratch came out instead. "Nothing is okay, Troylus. My dad is dead, and you're what? Fucking around? Coming into my bed when I'm asleep? How did you get in here?"

"No. That's not what I meant." He slid out of the bed and she backed away, slamming her back into the wet room door.

"Hey," Rullon said, making her head snap to the side and spot him sitting at the table with a bar in his hand halfway to his mouth. "Zellendine, I'm sorry if we startled you. And more than that, I'm sorry about your dad."

She curled over, her arms wrapping around a middle that felt like she had taken blow after blow.

But her mind was running full speed, trying to process this small part of her strange new reality.

"Why are you both here?" she asked, directing the question at Rullon.

"Leadership asked me. They didn't want you to be with strangers, and..." He looked over at Troylus and bit his lip. Putting the bar down in front of him, he turned to face her fully and frowned before he nodded and said, "They asked Briar's family first."

Even though she knew exactly how Briar felt recently, even though she knew it was for the best that she not push their carefully constructed boundary, and most of all, even though she wasn't even sure what she wanted out of her relationship with Briar anymore, him turning her away when she needed him most chipped off another piece of her heart.

"I," she started to say, her voice nothing more than a wheeze. She coughed, and started again, "Thank you."

Troylus stood next to the bed, wringing his hands in front of himself like he was itching to do something, but Rullon nodded and went back to his food.

She wasn't ready to start the conversation with Troylus about why he was in the bed with her. She wanted to remember everything from the night before and she needed to drink something before she was going to even try.

Going to the service, seeing her father's favorite treats, was like picking at a wound. She got herself something to eat and drink, although she doubted either would have any taste to her at the moment, she had work to do.

At the table, across from Rullon, Troylus awkwardly hovering about as if he couldn't figure out what to do with himself, she said the thought repeating in her head out loud.

"My father was killed on purpose, by someone with abilities. Someone with silver eyes."

Rullon squeezed his eyes shut, and hung his head.

Troylus stopped his fidgeting and stared at her, his breathing too fast, but he swallowed, and then nodded.

"You think so too."

"I don't see any other explanation. I'm sorry," Troylus said, his voice quiet with an almost anticipatory edge to it that made Zellendine pause.

"It's not your fault that someone with your eyes destroys people instead of fixing things," she said, and he relaxed against the bunk behind him, his breathing calming.

"We know that's what happened," Rullon said, nodding and opening his eyes. "But what do we do about it? Leadership has to know there's a problem now, there are more people with silver eyes all the time. They're going to be looking into this. I think maybe we should let them try and figure it out."

"For you, it may be enough to let them try and figure it out," she said, "To trust that they *will* figure it out and that they'll do anything about it. But I can't take the chance that they'll just look forward and pretend it didn't happen."

"So," Troylus said, standing up from his leaning position, "what are you planning to do?"

"First, I'm going to look at his holo. Then, I'm going to see my dad." She took a second to close her eyes and shove her feelings down into her toes before she went on. "Then, I'm going to find the fucker that did this and I'm going to make him pay."

2 2

TROYLUS

Whatever Troylus expected of Zellendine that day, it wasn't how she actually handled the tragedy.

She was so good with the people in the clinic after the accident, maybe that was why she was able to remain so singularly focused and work for her goal even though this loss was hers specifically. But he couldn't quite square the puddle of her, the screaming in agony version of her with this one. It was as if she allowed herself that, and now she was done with it and ready to do something, or several somethings.

Halfway through the day, he was taking food that Rullon had made to her, it was the third time she had eaten already.

Troylus couldn't help it, every time he saw the holo in her hands after looking away, the image of Stephen's outstretched hand flashed in his head.

Zellendine leaned forward from where she was sitting on the big bed, her hand reaching for the food, while she tapped something on the holo with her other hand.

She sucked in a breath and pulled her hand back, snatching the holo up off the bed and tapping something else. Her eyes grew gigantic, and a tremulous smile formed on her face. It was the first time she had smiled.

"Did you find something?" he asked, setting the food down on the bed next to her, not sitting himself like he wanted to because he still felt awkward about that morning.

"Yes," she said, looking up at him with her eyes heavy with tears waiting to fall.

"Are— " he cut himself off, he didn't want to ask if she was okay. He wasn't sure if he ever wanted to use the word again. "What's wrong?"

"Come here." She grabbed his hand and pulled, he stopped to pick up and move the food before he dropped onto it and made a mess.

Sitting next to her, she tapped away at the holo and pointed out something titled: Zellendine's Ongoing Notes.

"What does that have to do with anything? It looks like additional notes for a recently graduated apprentice. I have one too." The look on her face told him he was very wrong and had no idea what was in this one.

"Dad and I had a shared file called something entirely different. This wasn't here, this is new and..." she paused and tapped on the words. Before them were only two things. An odd sketch that didn't look like more than a cone and a dot as if it was only a beginning of something much larger. And a number.

"I don't get it. Is that something medics understand?"

"No. Dad was looking for a way for us to send the message. This is what we need to do that." She shut her eyes and hugged the holo to her chest. "Thank you, Dad."

He should have been happy, well, at least appreciative of what Stephen had managed to uncover.

But all he could focus on at the moment was the very real possibility that Stephen had died for the information she held in her hand.

"Zellendine," he said, the sadness in his own voice surprised even him. He wasn't sure pointing out what he thought explicitly for her was such a good idea. "Do you think it's safe to have that holo? Maybe it would be best to try and hide it."

"I…" She looked back and forth from the holo in her hands to Troylus, her face going from clear happiness to sadness to resolve.

"No," she said. "You're right. I'll memorize it, and then I'll put the holo back in the clinic."

She ran her hand along the edge of the holo in a loving, soft caress. His heart ached watching her.

He was haunted by that outstretched hand, but she was hanging on to this, the last thing her father touched while he was alive. Of all the things he thought he could help her through, he understood finally, that learning how to let go of this small thing, was something she was going to have to do on her own.

All he could do to help, would be to protect her while she had this terrible risk in her possession.

"How much time do I have left to be with him before…" Her voice trailed off, but Troylus, and he suspected his dad too by the small flinch that crossed his face, understood what she meant.

"No rush," Rullon said. "After the accident, everything is a bit behind. So, you can take whatever time you need."

When she was ready, they went with her. Their cobbled together collection of people left from other broken families, they formed their own family-like unit.

Zellendine spent an entire day with the sheet-covered body of her father, both Troylus and Rullon by her side.

There were some tears, but mostly she told them stories.

She ran her fingers along the sheet where it covered her father's good hand, and she spoke of when her mother was alive. She spoke of her apprenticeship. She spoke of all the small and large things about her dad that came into her head in the moment.

Neither of them said a thing about her looking back. The only time it was allowed was during the mourning period. And even if it had been prohibited, Troylus didn't give a fuck anymore.

Whatever rules the Chapter had were only a concern to him in the threat they posed, but soon he would be on the planet, and as soon as Rullon and Zellendine were with him, he planned on never following their rules again.

If someone like Stephen, who followed the rules almost every day of his life and only broke them in the service of others, was going to die for that small transgression, then the Chapter was beyond repair.

He touched the edge of the sheet, not sure if he was actually making contact with the man beneath it or not, but he wanted to promise him.

Regardless of how hard it was going to be, or what he would have to do to make it happen, Troylus promised Stephen he would protect Zellendine and that after they got on the planet, he was going to do everything he could to take down the Chapter so they couldn't do what they did to Stephen again.

23

ZELLENDINE

Watching her father being sent into the stars was so much worse than she thought it was going to be. She had in her head that somehow seeing him sent out of the chute would be a kind of catharsis. That it would somehow magically provide an end to her grief.

She was wrong.

The pain in her heart lingered as she, Troylus, and Rullon finally lost sight of him and then walked away. The missing piece of her life, the giant gaping hole that was normally filled with her father, was still as empty and black with just as much gravitational pull as before.

Part of her wanted to compare it to when her mother died, but she was much younger then, and there was so much she had pushed out of her mind to allow herself to move on that there were big patches of missing memory.

But at least she had the holo in her hand. At least she had the number to memorize. At least she had a mission.

"It was radiation," she said, once they were all back in their quarters and she was eating another helping of Rullon's food.

"What was radiation?" Rullon asked, pausing with a bite halfway to his mouth.

"One of the things that Stephen found when he scanned me was that my cells had responded to some kind of highly focused and apparently benign radiation," Troylus said, sitting on a small stool he had pulled over to the table to act like a chair.

"Yes, but that same radiation reading was on my dad's wounds." She stared off into space for a moment, one hand feeding herself, the other tapping a steady beat on the holo beside her.

"So, it was for sure one of us who did it." Troylus didn't ask the question, he said it as a statement of fact.

"How did you find that out?" Rullon asked.

"While we were in there with my dad, below the table I had his holo run scans." She was still staring into the middle distance, tapping away on the edge of the holo she used, but she looked back at them, just in time to notice as Rullon's jowls grew more pronounced and a line appeared between his brows.

Rullon looked to Troylus who just nodded in response.

"What?" she asked, looking back and forth between them.

"I'm just letting him know that, yes, that makes sense to me," Troylus said, "And that he should consider people like me dangerous."

"Stop it," she said, shaking her head and bopping Troylus on the shoulder as she stood up to get something to drink. "We already know that you're not dangerous. Some people probably can't control themselves, like whoever exploded and killed themselves and a bunch of others. But not everyone is a good person, so the likelihood that someone who developed abilities would turn out to be fucking horrible was high as long as more people were getting silver."

"Getting silver?" Troylus asked, he said it like the combination of words felt wrong and clunky in his mouth.

"I don't have a good way to say it. Until we come up with something, we'll all just have to know what we mean."

"A good way to say it," Rullon said, shaking his head. "Even that doesn't sound good. It sounds like this is a disease. Are we sure this won't make people sick in the long run? And do we have any idea where the radiation is coming from?"

"You're right," Zellendine said, bringing her drink back to the table. "It doesn't sound great, but no. It all seems to be beneficial side effects. And also no, I know dad was going to do some testing all over the ship, to try and find the source of the radiation. Some of those scans are still up on his holo, but as far as I can tell he didn't find anything. If he had, I think he would have kept the scan, or at least mentioned it in that secret message file to me."

While the guys talked about theories on the source of the radiation, Zellendine put it out of her mind to focus on who she thought could have been responsible for her father's death.

Of all the things she didn't know, there was one thing she did, where she found his body.

So, the next day she was going to make her way to that hallway, to that room. She was going to make note of her surroundings in ways she hadn't before. And maybe, if she got lucky, she would find something.

The only question left in her plan was how she was going to make sure Troylus didn't follow her.

24

TROYLUS

She was up to something. He knew she was scheming. She was going inside herself, and she was keeping something secret. He couldn't be mad, because maybe it was just how she was compartmentalizing to save herself from her own grief. But he couldn't help thinking she was up to something that was going to get her hurt.

There were silver-eyed people all over the place. Their abilities were volatile. He didn't trust anyone anyway, and right at that moment he wanted to keep all the people he cared about hidden away from everyone else.

What good was his ability if he couldn't use it to help protect people?

"I'm heading to the clinic," she said after getting ready in the morning and grabbing her dad's holo.

"Are you putting that away in the clinic?" he asked, popping the last bite of food into his mouth.

She looked at the holo as if it were a lot more than a standard issue device many had used over the years. Part of him wanted to tell her to hang onto it, but it was as dangerous to her where leadership was concerned, as it was sentimental to her personally.

But she nodded. She folded her arms around it and nodded to both he and his dad, and then she was gone to brave the hallways.

"I should walk her to the clinic," Troylus said.

"You can't escort her everywhere," Rullon said, slapping his hand on his shoulder and passing him for his turn in the wet room.

"Fine. But I can't stand around. I'm going to the office." Rullon nodded as he shut the wet room door and Troylus left, diving into the human chaos that the hallways had become.

No matter what Rullon said, or that he knew he was starting to piss Zellendine off by being too there all the time, Troylus still scanned the people ahead of him, trying to pick her out of the crowd. Often, it worked. He could usually spot her, but not that time.

She's fine, he said inside his head.

Of all the places she should be okay, the clinic was one. He just had to keep telling himself she was going to make it to the clinic just fine. No one was going to mess with her on the way there.

Nope, everything was going to be fine. They had all been through enough, they just had to make it to the planet.

But no matter how many times he repeated assurances in his head, he didn't entirely believe it.

The only positive thing about the madness of the hallways, was that by the time he got to the starwalker office, his worries were pushed to the back of his brain by his overwhelming urge to punch people in the throat who had forgotten how to walk.

"Hey, how is she?" Parmita asked. He appreciated her not bothering with small talk and bullshit.

"I don't know, Princess." He raked a hand through his hair,

trying to prepare himself for a day of work. "She seems like she's dealing with it, but I don't know what's happening in her head and I don't know what it looks like to deal with shit right, you know?"

She nodded, but he wasn't sure she did know what he meant. No one onboard really knew what dealing with shit right looked like. Not even the medics did much beyond trying to help people keep moving forward because that's all that mattered to everyone.

But he didn't want Zellendine to get hard and angry like he did after his mom died. The problem was, he didn't understand another way to respond when everyone around you pretended like your loss never happened after a little while.

"How are the repairs going?" he asked, shaking his head and trying to focus on what he was supposed to.

"Well, the outside is almost done. And then we're all going to be trying to fix that section on the inside, and I have no idea where we're going to get the parts, or how long that disaster is going to take." She slumped, grabbing her suit and allowing him to help her into it.

"Do you want help out there?" he asked.

"Yeah, it would be good to have a dumbass out there with me. Imogene needs a break anyway." She smiled at him as he helped her with her helmet.

"Imogene has been out there a lot, huh?" he asked, getting his own suit and waving down another starwalker to help him get into it.

"She's been out there so much I'm not sure when she's slept." Parmita leaned against the wall while he finished getting in his suit.

The semi constant presence of Imogene made sense to him, but it didn't surprise him that Parmita didn't get it. He wondered how she managed to keep her ability a secret while she helped with the last of the fixes that they had left for the regular crew to work on.

Going through the airlock wasn't as bad as it used to be, but he was looking forward to getting on the planet when the concept of outside didn't include threat of death from breathing.

"Hey, Princess, have we heard anything about who is going to be on what spindle? And who is going to be auxiliary support crew for us?" Troylus asked, pulling himself along on the hand holds while she released her little air puffs beside him.

"No, we haven't heard a thing. And, you know they just put things in the computer, and it tells them what to do. So I don't know why they're waiting so damn long."

In the past, he would have agreed with her. But maybe this time, they were watching everything and they hadn't made a decision about how to handle it all yet.

Maybe they were going to try and send all the silver eyed people down to the surface with the starwalkers. That made sense to him, but he hoped that somehow, he would be able to get Zellendine and Rullon assigned to his spindle. In a perfect universe he would be able to hand-pick all the people he was assigned to create a burgh with, but if he could only pick two, it was definitely her and his dad.

The question was, how to make that happen.

25

———

ZELLENDINE

FEW PEOPLE WERE DOWN THAT HALLWAY. THE ONE THAT SHE would always think of with an asterisk in her mind. The hallway where *it* happened. But she had to think about it as a place to find clues. She had to pay attention and put aside the visions that flashed in her head from just being near this place.

She had to keep her gaze off that spot.

The door to the room where she found him was no longer in place. Why it had been removed, she couldn't fathom. She didn't remember it being burnt, but it may have been.

Just inside, her step was uneven and she wobbled, but it looked like the room was a small meeting space with three chairs and a low table.

No wonder she didn't know about this room, why would space like this be wasted on a small meeting room?

And, more importantly, who had her father been meeting?

Moving further inside, she looked under the chairs, the table, inspected the corners, and every nook and cranny she could find. But there was nothing to lead her toward an answer, nothing to give her even a next step in her search. Nothing.

She stood in the entryway to the room, looking back at the chairs, trying to imagine her father in there, talking to someone, blissfully unaware of what was about to happen to him.

Of all the possibilities of how it might have happened, the one where he didn't know it was coming, the one where it happened so fast that he didn't have time to even be afraid was the only one she could stomach.

Falling to the ground a second later, she thought maybe her legs had given out from grief. But no, someone had shoved her.

She landed, hard, on her hands and knees and looked behind her just as a foot connected with her stomach, lifting her off the ground with the force of the kick and knocking the breath from her lungs.

"You duplicitous bitch." Briar's voice was low and grinding. His silver eyes shone with more than hate, it was revulsion and disgust, rage, and self-righteousness.

Coughing, she tried to suck down enough air to ask him what the fuck he was talking about.

"Don't come anywhere near my family again." Briar leaned down close to her face while she gasped for breath and held an arm to the pain in her abdomen.

He didn't seem to notice anything wrong with her beyond the kind of careful observation her dad got when he was studying something in the clinic.

There was no sign of their history in his eyes in that moment. The only thing present was the eerie examination like she was a sample he found only mildly interesting beyond what it could tell him about something else.

Finally, she got enough air.

"Briar." She meant to say more, but her first words were drowned by her lungs ability to inflate. With more work to breathe and him leaning even closer, she tried again. "Fuck you, Briar. What the fuck is wrong with you?" She wanted to pick up the table and bash him in the head with it. She wanted to lash out at him like he had at her, only her attack would be in self-defense and not totally unprovoked. But she could barely get the words out and they were enough to leave her struggling again.

"Oh, nice. So, there's something wrong with me, but you're just a perfect person. Right, Zelle?" He reared back and balled his hands into fists.

She managed to sit up and tuck part of her body behind one of the chairs.

"Don't call me that." Her voice sounded close to yelling, but it was actually the only way to force her body to breathe without wheezing, with big, forceful inhales and exhales.

"I can't call you a name I gave you? Why not? You just want to cut all ties with me?"

For a second he sounded almost normal, almost like the guy she had always known. For a second she thought the walls the silver had built around his memories were starting to fall like Troylus's had.

But then he sneered and kicked the table at her.

It tumbled through the room and slammed into her side as she ducked her head. The metal of the table made a hollow bong sound, and pain shot up from her side and back to make her vision blurry.

"Stop, Briar," she yelled, her body aching and her mind whirling, trying to come up with a way out of this situation.

Her eyes couldn't help themselves anymore, she looked at the place on the floor where her father's body was.

A singed mark, at least not a clear outline of his body, was deep and dark on the floor. Her wobble from earlier made sense and her body let her know there was no more she could do to prevent meeting his same fate if Briar had flames as his ability.

She vomited down the side of the chair, the noxious chunks dripped down onto the floor.

"You're not worth it. You're disgusting. I'll let leadership deal with you," Briar said, his voice devoid of anything other than exhaustion, and he turned and left her there, with the smell of puke in her nostrils, and pain everywhere.

Hollower, in so many more ways than she was when she set out to find clues, and not any richer in that regard, she lifted a shaking hand to swipe at her mouth.

Fine, he didn't want her to see Upton anymore, but it wasn't up to him. It was up to his dads.

And she was going to do her duty by her little friend.

If she couldn't help her father's memory yet, she was going to do what he would have wanted.

26

TROYLUS

"This sealer isn't going to be enough." Parmita cocked her head to one side and then the other, studying her work on a seam of the cobbled together exterior of the blown-out part of the ship.

"What do you think? Will it hold?" She asked, turning toward where he was shoving at a panel, trying to force it back to flat.

"Sure, it will. Come over here and help me with this and then I'll check your seal work," Troylus said.

Yeah, he would check it and then he would ensure it did work no matter how much it wouldn't have before.

"Fine." She rolled her shoulders and slipped the container of sealant into a pocket on the side of her suit.

"How is it going out there?" Rullon's voice came over his comm, sounding oddly chipper.

"Okay." Troylus spoke carefully, it wasn't like his dad to sound so... fake happy.

Parmita tapped the side of her helmet and pointed at Troylus so he did the same, cutting his comm.

"What the hell was that?" She asked.

So he wasn't wrong. That was weird.

"No idea. Maybe we should check about coming in and finishing this later?" He tapped his comm again and bit his lip for a second while he tried to hear anything in the background that would explain it.

"Rullon, should we head in and make a plan, or keep at this?" There, that sounded reasonable and appropriate, no matter who was listening.

"Actually, that's a good idea. We need to get more parts out there anyway, I think." His voice still had that bizarre false quality to it, and the hairs on Troylus's arms stood on end.

"Come on, Princess," he said, and Parmita nodded, using the air bursts to push herself ahead of him toward the air lock.

Troylus tried not to imagine all manner of issues as the air lock cycled through. He failed.

Was he going to walk into another trial for someone? Was there another accident and more people were dead? Was Zellendine a screaming puddle of grief somewhere and he needed to go get her back to quarters? He had no idea, but his stomach had turned into a rock while he waited to find out.

Finally, the air lock opened on a shuffling crowd of starwalkers, they shot furtive glances toward the office and Imogene was the only one to step forward and help him out of his suit, moving on to Parmita once she was done with him. She didn't say a word, but the hard look in her eye told Troylus that he wasn't wrong. This was not a pleasant interruption.

In the office, the only starwalker present was Rullon. But he wasn't alone in there.

Standing next to him, looming over his chair, was a member of leadership from another shift, whose name Troylus didn't know.

On Rullon's other side, Alara sat, leaning back in her seat, showing no sign that her visit was anything other than a cordial social call.

"Alara," Troylus said, nodding his head to recognize her presence and nodding to the unknown person as well. "I don't know that I've ever seen leadership down here."

She smiled a sweet and soft smile that didn't meet her eyes and tilted her head to the side. "You know, I think you might be right that we don't connect often enough with the starwalkers. I think we spend more time in the way of all the other crews. To be fair, most of us are afraid of the thought of going into space with nothing but a suit."

Her chuckle at her own attempt at self deprecation was alone, the sound of it not matching the silent trepidation hanging thick in the room.

"Well, what prompted this visit?" He smiled back at her, a lazy smile he hoped didn't tell her much, and leaned against the wall. "Do you want an update on the repairs to the hole in the ship? Because that project is pretty big."

"Oh, no. We trust you all are working very diligently to make that happen as soon as possible." She waved her hand in the air, as if the accident and the horrible aftermath weren't still being felt in more than just the closing of a section of hallway and massive hole blown in the ship.

He waited for her to say more. He wasn't going to do what she wanted, which was start blabbering about nothing and get himself in trouble in the process. They were good at this, the game he thought all the leadership crew played. But he was going to be better. He had to be. He had too many secrets.

Finally, she blew out a pent-up breath and sighed,

"Troylus, I suppose I should just get to my questions."

"You have questions for me?"

She cut her glance to Rullon and then back to him. He didn't take the bait and look at his dad. Whatever she wanted to ask him, Rullon would have found a way to put her off until he was there. He knew his dad well enough to know he wouldn't have screwed up and offered any information that would have set Troylus even further back in this conversation than he already was.

"More than a few."

"Okay, go for it."

"First, I wanted to check on Zellendine. How is she doing?" Alara looked sincere, but he didn't trust anyone in her position.

"As well as can be expected. She wants to try and focus on moving forward, but at a time like this… it's sometimes hard to make your brain do that." There was more leeway for people just after a loss, and Alara had known Stephen, so when her face fell and she nodded, he thought he hadn't hurt Zellendine by letting her know. Hopefully, it would buy Zellendine a little more time to process before leadership expected too much from her.

"Understandable, given the circumstances." Alara shuffled her hands in her lap, a small adjustment that made it clear to Troylus how much she was a true believer in the Chapter motto. Only someone wholly indoctrinated would have been uncomfortable by their not really mention of something that had only happened a few days before.

"Second," she said, looking back up from her hands to him, "I was wondering how you came to be in the area to find Zellendine and bring her back to your quarters?"

Huh? What the hell was she getting at?

"I was just walking the halls, trying to get used to how crammed everyone is, and saw her. She's one of the only people I can easily pick out of the crowds." It wasn't a lie. But he was sure as hell not going to tell Alara about the conversation with Imogene and their abilities.

Alara's eyes narrowed just a fraction.

Shit, he said something wrong. He didn't know what it was, but her reaction couldn't have been good.

"Third, do you enjoy having her be a part of your quarters?"

"It's a little strange, it's easier to ignore a stranger in a weird way than someone you've known all your life." How was she expecting him to answer that? That he wanted to be with Zellendine all the time and that he didn't trust anyone else not to turn silver and get angry with her for no damn reason like had? No. Alara was the last person he wanted to know that.

"But do you enjoy her being there? I know you two have been struggling with your friendship, but then I hear about you coming to her aid and becoming roommates."

"Well, Stephen was a good person. And anyone in her situation, seeing that, it couldn't have been easy. Maybe I'm just not as much of a jerk as I thought I was. Rullon made the decision to move quarters, to help her out."

Alara was dangerously close to looking back to last shift, her cagey language didn't lessen the shock that ran through him knowing she wasn't looking forward about this.

"Hmmm. That's true. And I have never thought you were a jerk."

Yeah, sure she hadn't. Well, he wasn't going to call her out on her thoughts about him, but he did raise an eyebrow.

"Last, I would like to know if you were the one that killed Stephen," she said, her face betraying neither the fact that she was full on looking back now, nor the fact that she had just insinuated that he was a killer.

"No." He wasn't going to elaborate or let her think she was ever going to get him to admit to something he didn't do. He curled his hands into fists and crossed his arms over his chest, the guy standing next to her stood up a little straighter and braced himself.

Asshole. That guy thought puffing himself up was going to intimidate him? He could go get bent.

"Good. Thank you for your time. I hope the repairs continue to go well." She stood up from her seat and walked out of the room, the asshole on her tail.

He looked at Rullon, whose face was set in hard lines emphasized with every grind of his jaw.

"We need to talk," his dad said, low and harsh, as soon as they were well beyond hearing.

Yes, they clearly did. And he needed to come up with a plan if leadership was aiming their inquiry into Stephen's death at him.

ZELLENDINE

Knocking on Briar's door, coming here at all, she knew was a risk. But he wasn't going to attack her in front of his dads. And she needed to know if it was just him, or if their whole family didn't want her around anymore.

The door swung open and Journo's smile dropped into soft eyes and a sympathetic frown as he shook his head.

"Oh, Zellendine, I'm so sorry about Stephen, he is a very special man and will be sorely missed."

She bit her lip and nodded, tasting a trickle of blood she bit down so hard, but it helped to keep from crying. Journo managed to give his condolences in the perfect Chapter way, looking forward to the times her dad wasn't going to be there, but she wanted to yell, was. Her dad was a very special man. The present tense around him made it hurt even worse. In reality there was never going to be a present for him again.

"Thank you. How is Upton doing?" Her voice managed to remain steady, even if it was devoid of feeling. That was the best she could do.

"Much better actually. Your treatment did wonders, but you

can wait if you want to do further treatment. He seems to be doing well, and I know you may need some time."

"Yes, that may be true. But you don't want me to stop checking up on him entirely, right?" It was an awkward question, but she needed a direct answer, not one that would leave doubt in her mind.

"Of course we want you to keep treating him. Look how much better he is already. Hey, come in really quick and see him. I think that would make you feel better." Journo swung the door further open and she stepped inside, nodding at him as she passed.

Upton was sitting at the table, a holo in front of him with work she recognized from her days learning at his age.

"Hey, Buddy. How are you feeling?" she asked, standing next to him and taking in his improved coloring and the fact he was out of bed and seemed to not need to be buried in blankets anymore. That was already an improvement.

"I'm better, but…" he stopped what he was doing and looked up at her, his little face full of sympathy and pain, water building in his eyes. "How are you?"

"Better now that I can see you're doing well. I'm sorry I didn't come for a little bit. I, um, well, there were things I had to do. But I think I'll be back in a few days again, to check on you. Would that be okay?"

He nodded, the threat of tears gone and she smiled.

"Zellendine." His voice took on a haunting timber, his eyes unfocused and stared into the middle between them, he was a thousand light years away again. "Be careful. It wants all of you who can't be one, dead. You don't belong here."

She felt all the hairs on her arms stand, her heart thudded in her chest and her stomach flipped over.

"What wants me dead?" She asked, her throat dry and the words sticking in it as she did.

"Everything."

Journo jumped forward and touched his son's shoulder. Upton collapsed into his arms, blinking and sweating.

He looked up at Zellendine and a tear did fall then.

"I'm sorry," he said, then he shivered. "I'm cold, Dad."

"Zellendine, I think maybe we should have a different medic look out for him from now on," Journo said, his voice hard.

She couldn't speak. She definitely couldn't argue, she just nodded and left.

At least he knew what he had to do to get Upton warm again. But she had no idea how to explain to him that it wasn't her influence that had done this to his son. It had to be the silver in his eye.

But that still didn't explain where the silver was coming from, or why he said everything wanted her dead. Or who he meant when he said, all of you who can't be one.

She walked down the hall, not realizing until she was halfway to the other side of the ship, that she had no where to go.

28

TROYLUS

Rullon was right. He slammed shut the door of their quarters, needing to be anywhere but there, faced with how right he was.

Leadership was going to try and pin Stephen's murder on him. And he had no idea how to stop them.

There wouldn't be a last minute save at a trial for him. It didn't matter that Zellendine knew he didn't do it. It didn't matter that Rullon knew, or anyone else. He didn't have a good answer to where he was or even why he was in that corridor when she found the body.

Even if he had a good answer, there was no reason to think they wouldn't have done the same to him anyway.

If he had known his own standing up for Zellendine during her trial would have put a target on his back, he still would have done it, but maybe he could have done other things differently to make it less likely. Maybe.

He rubbed his hands over his face and through his hair, not caring that one of his elbows caught someone's arm as he stormed through the crowds in the halls.

Where could he even go to get away from everyone to think through it all?

Of all the places that flashed in his head, the orchard was the only option he thought might have a chance to be empty enough to suit his needs.

Fine, the orchard was the first place he would try.

Damn it. He wanted to find Zellendine. He wanted to lock himself away with her in their quarters and hope they would be able to wait out whatever bullshit inquiry that leadership was running.

The orchard was quiet. At least it was always that. Even when there were people tucked in and amongst the trees, everyone had the decency to stay quiet and calm. Or maybe it was the trees that inspired people to be as still as possible.

It didn't matter if it was caused by the people or by the environment, it was still his favorite place onboard.

He wandered between the trees, seeing few people, which let his heart slow, his fists unclench, and his stomach undo the knots in it.

Rounding a trunk of a tree, heading into the little clearing he thought of as his own, a bird glided by in front of him.

Everything about it made him want to sit down and wait until he saw another one, but he continued on, hoping his clearing would give him even more chances to see birds. If he was lucky, another pair might have even built another nest.

Of all the things that had happened onboard the ship in the last shift and this one, the birds nesting were one of the best.

Zellendine sat below the tree that used to hold the baby birds, a holo in her hands, her fingers tapping away, while she chewed on her lip.

He moved into the clearing and neared her side, but she still didn't notice his presence.

It wasn't until he sat down beside her that her head popped up, her eyes widening, a wavering smile forming on her face.

She dropped the holo into her lap and flung her arms around his neck.

"Are you okay?" he asked, hugging her back.

Not that he was complaining, but it wasn't like her to be so eager to hang onto him. And with what she had been going through, he hoped she wasn't reliving something to freshen her grief.

"Troylus," she said. Just his name.

It hit the part of him that wanted to hide from leadership, the part of him that wanted to pretend everything was going to be fine. It made all his deepest emotions as tender as they had ever been and he buried his face in her hair, hugging her tighter.

She squeaked, a sharp, quick sound of pain.

He pulled back from her and barely touched her arms as he held her out from him. His eyes looked over every part of her he could see, but there was no obvious sign of injury.

"What's wrong?"

"I..." she trailed off, looking down at where her hands dropped into her lap. "I went to see the room where he died."

Equal parts fury and a desperate need to make it better raged in him as she told him about Briar attacking her.

"Zellendine, listen, I know you don't want to do anything about this, but you need to tell leadership," he said when she was done as he ran a hand along her cheek.

"But they might keep him onboard, not let him colonize. This isn't entirely his fault. It's whatever is happening to him from the ability showing up. You know that." Her eyes were begging him to let it go, to just accept that her decision was to protect Briar, but he couldn't.

"No, it is his fault. Even with the ability doing what it does, he still has a choice in how he responds to it. I didn't hit you, even when it was making me furious with you. I tried to shove all that away." She shook her head, and he couldn't even blame her. He had made excuses for the way he treated her. He was the reason she was so willing to forgive Briar. He had overcome it, so she was hoping Briar would too.

He tucked her, gently, into his chest, his chin resting on her head and his arms around her.

There was no phenomenon in the universe that he could think of that would make him hurt her the way Briar had. And he wanted to kill Briar for it. For a minute, he was more than willing to be the kind of person leadership thought he was.

"I just want to pretend he doesn't exist," she mumbled.

Did he hear her right?

Tilting her chin up with his hand, pulling his head back so he could look into her eyes, he waited for her to take it back.

"Are you serious?" His voice was rough. Low and soft, but rough, because his out of control heart beat was back and he ached for her to mean what he thought she meant.

One corner of her mouth turned up and she looked down at his lips before she leaned in and kissed him.

The emotions ricocheting through his body took conscious effort to keep from flying out of his hands in his blue light. But he held them back, until she deepened the kiss and climbed onto his lap.

"Wait," he said, leaving her lips behind and putting his forehead to hers.

She laughed, a tiny giggle.

"I'm sorry, I got carried away."

"No," he said, looking at her and shaking his head, a wide ridiculous smile on his face. "Don't be sorry, I am that I don't have control of this stupid blue light yet."

She nodded, but she broke eye contact and he couldn't help but kick himself that he couldn't just be normal.

"Zellendine," he said, his throat dry, one hand reaching up to cup her cheek, "If I didn't have this damn ability I would carry you back to quarters right now."

Her dark brown eyes crinkled at the corners, mischievous glee dancing in their depths.

"We share quarters," she said.

"Yes," he said, carefully. Oh, so carefully, because if she said too much he might just explode in blue light without her lips on his.

"Maybe we should try to see how much control you have."

They met each other, she didn't kiss him, and he didn't kiss her, they kissed each other in their perfect little clearing.

They kissed until someone hit Troylus in the back with a thick branch.

29

ZELLENDINE

"No, Briar, stop it," Zellendine yelled, jumping up from Troylus and grabbing at the branch in Briar's hands.

He stared at her over the length of the wood, it's rough bark digging into her palms as he tried to wrench it away from her.

"You fucking bitch," he said, his voice little more than a growl.

"Ahhh," Troylus groaned, crawling away from Briar, his head hanging.

"What the fuck is wrong with you? You just attacked your best friend," she yelled, yanking on the wood and finally pulling it away from him.

"Wrong with me? You're the one coming between us, you. It's all you, destroying everything." Briar balled his hands into fists, closed his eyes, and sucked down air through his nose, his teeth bared and clenched.

"Briar, fuck off. Just go," she said, trying not to take her eyes off of Briar as Troylus leaned against a tree trunk, touching his back over one shoulder, grimacing as he did.

"I don't need to listen to you," Briar yelled, his eyes popping open and his hands opening and closing on fists.

"You don't have to, but you should." Troylus said, shoving himself up to standing, keeping a hand on the tree.

His every move looked like it hurt, but his face said he didn't care and was more than willing to punch Briar in the face.

"Come on, Troylus. You hate her. Don't let her get to you." Briar turned to face Troylus, his face changing completely in the process, as if he was a switch that flipped when he wasn't looking at her.

"I have never hated her, and I sure as hell don't now. You don't even know her," Troylus said, pushing off from the tree and coming to stand just in front of Zellendine, his hands out at his sides, wide open.

She looked back and forth between them, watching as they said nothing but their hands said everything.

Troylus was ready. His hands, where the blue light came from, were prepared to do whatever he needed.

Briar was still closing and opening his, like confusion was flaring inside him and his hands were responding.

"He doesn't want to hurt us," she said, her voice low, but Briar's head snapped to look at her.

She tightened her grip on the branch, raising it into place in case she needed to swing it at him. He sneered.

"Yes, I want to hurt you, just not Troylus. Unless..." Briar turned his gaze back to Troylus standing next to her, his eyes narrowing and his hands flaring open. "Unless you're gone to her side."

"I will always be on her side," Troylus said, raising his hands out in front of him as if he was going to throw the blue light at Briar right that second.

"She isn't one of us. She needs to die." Briar's voice was high and warbled in pitch, like he was losing control.

"Come on, Troylus. Let's just go," she said, using one hand to pull on the sleeve of his uniform while she kept the branch aloft with the other.

"No. He needs to get his ass kicked or he'll keep coming after you." Troylus sounded like they were talking about what they were going to eat that night, but the meaning of his words hit her anyway. She didn't think he was wrong.

"You want her dead, you'll have to kill me first." Troylus took a step closer to Briar who stumbled as he stepped back.

"No, I can't use it on you," Briar said, taking one last hate filled look at Zellendine and then darting back into the trees. The sound of his retreat bounced off of the woods around them, assuring her he was actually leaving.

Zellendine threw the branch and wiped her palms on her uniform.

"I need to go after him," Troylus said, turning back to her, one of his hands over his shoulder again and slumping as he looked at her.

"What you need, is to come with me to quarters where I can look at how bad your back is." She took his hand and led him through the orchard.

He followed along willingly, but she was sure he felt the tension running through her.

It wasn't even from the threats, or Briar's attack, it was from how similar his statement about her not being one of them and needing to die was to the cryptic things Upton said.

Abilities were one thing, no matter how fantastic, even abilities tied to emotions that caused some major conflict issues, including among people you knew and loved. But some kind of mandate that those who were different needed to be killed?

She wasn't ready to process all the implications of her being a target of the ugliest of the side effects of whatever was happening.

But she didn't have much of a choice. Briar, maybe more than Briar, wanted her dead. And someone had already killed her dad.

Troylus rubbed a thumb over the back of her hand as they moved through the masses in the halls, it was enough to remind her not to panic. She had a very powerful person on her side. And his blue light.

30

TROYLUS

By the time they reached quarters, there was blood trickling down his back from the place on his shoulder blade where Briar's damn stick had gouged him.

The attack was going to leave bruises, and it had knocked the wind out of him, but the blood was really going to piss him off.

He watched as Zellendine shut their door behind him and all he wanted to do was take her in his arms and test out his control. But she was never going to let that happen as long as he was bleeding.

"Fuck Briar," he said, and Zellendine laughed a humorless laugh before putting her hands over her face.

"Just so we're one hundred percent clear, because I don't want you to believe whatever sick shit he says about me," she started, pulling her hands from her face and looking right at him, "I was never going to partner with anyone until I knew for sure."

He laughed and rubbed the hand of his good shoulder roughly through his hair.

"Yeah, and you were sure about him. I get it," he said, backing up to the table and plopping down onto a chair.

"Don't worry, Zellendine. I know you two have been together for a long time and I shouldn't have tried to get between you for long. I'm sure he'll get over it like I did." He closed his eyes and rubbed at the back of his neck and the knot forming there. He was lying his ass off, and he didn't want her to know.

He opened his eyes and she was inches from his face, one of her brows high and her hands on her hips, bent at the waist, leaning over him.

"Shit," he mumbled, sitting back and pulling his face from hers.

"Will you stop being a fucking moron." She grabbed his hand and pulled him to his feet, dragging him behind her to the wet room.

"Listen," she said, undoing the top of his uniform.

"Hey," he said, twisting away from her deft fingers.

"No. This is my assignment. I need to see it." She turned him back to her and he dropped his hands. Yes, she was a medic, and he needed one, no matter what it was doing to him to have her undressing him.

"As I was saying." She looked up at him after undoing the top of his uniform again and the look she gave him was like he was small and being scolded by someone.

"People assumed Briar and I would partner, we talked about it, I assumed that at some point it would happen. But we never made the commitment. And I was never going to until I got to the planet because people can change." She shot him another look, one even more pointed than the last, and she went around him to his back, sucking in her breath with a hiss when she got there.

It must have looked even worse than he realized.

She placed a gentle hand on his back, managing to avoid any place that would make him hurt anymore than he already did.

He closed his eyes and hoped that it wouldn't be the only way in which she would touch him from now on, like one of her patients.

"You're right." Her voice broke his heart, it wasn't sad, it was cautiously happy.

If she was feeling that way about her future with Briar after what he had done to her and to Troylus, he was never going to be able to have her in his life for very long. He was just a temporary fill in while Briar got his head out of his ass.

"He never knew me," she said, making him snap his eyes open and turn around to face her.

She was smiling at him, her face unguarded and daring.

"That idiot thinks you're a lot of things you're not, but I shouldn't have done the same damn thing," he said, reaching out a hand to run it along her cheek.

"Oh?" She raised her eyebrow at him again and he laughed while he nodded.

"Yeah. No one makes you do anything you don't want to unless it's a requirement for survival."

He moved in closer to her and his heart lost its rhythm as she ran her hands up his chest.

"So, you want to try and test my control."

Zellendine wrapped her arms around his neck and pulled his mouth down to hers.

Their kiss was deep and long, he never wanted it to end, but at least he didn't think his hands were going to explode by the time she pulled back from his mouth and looked into his eyes.

"But first, I need to treat you, and then talk you through treating me."

He growled and buried his face in her neck, nuzzling and kissing the soft skin where it curved to meet her shoulder.

"Ah, so you want to try and test my control," she said, her voice breathless, and it happened.

Blue light floated up out of his palms, it coiled around them and licked at his back and all along her body.

She arched and twisted, crying out in pain, and he pulled the light back, tucking his palms into his sides, swearing he would never touch her again if that was what it took to protect her.

"Zellendine, I'm so sorry. No. Oh, shit." He was stammering and his arms flapped around while he tried to keep his hands planted and safe against his own legs.

"No," she said, bending over double, bracing herself with her hands on her knees, she waved one hand in the air and took deep breaths.

"What can I do? I'll go. I'll move rooms."

"Stop, Troylus." She stood up, putting a hand to her side and starting to undo her uniform with frenzied fingers.

"Don't. Please, I don't want to hurt you again." He brought his hands out to stop hers, but shoved them back at his sides again, shaking his head.

"Look at my back and my side please," she said, placing a hand on his arm which sent a shiver down his spine.

"I'm not sure..."

"Do it." She turned and pulled down her uniform, showing him the exposed skin of the area he pressed too hard on in the orchard that made her flinch away from him.

But there was no sign of injury, no sign of issue at all.

"You're fine. It all looks great. Now, come on, I should get out of here." He went to move past her and she grabbed him, turning him around to face her.

"Troylus, you did this." Her eyes were alight, bright and shining in the depths of the deep brown of them.

"I know, I hurt you. I'm sorry, I just don't see any sign of it. If it's too deep we should take you to the clinic. Come on."

He turned again and she clamped her hand on his arm, forcing his focus back to her.

"Listen. It was probably black and blue, I might have had broken ribs. That's how bad I was hurt before. But this," she said, twisting to make him look at her clear back again. "This is because of your blue light. You don't just fix things on the ship. You fixed me."

Opening and closing his mouth, the words failing him, Troylus struggled to accept that he was capable of something that incredible.

"Healed you?" he managed to say, his hands releasing their tight hold on his uniform at his sides. "How?"

"I have no idea." She reached up to touch his cheek, to run her other hand along his chest and stomach, it sent his body into a strange need to get her closer and push her away at the same time. Part of him couldn't accept that he had done something positive for her instead of the hurt he thought he had caused. And part of him wanted to be back to normal so he could be with her the way his whole body longed for.

But in the end, he kept his hands to himself, only allowing himself to look at her, and to kiss her before he pulled back and bit his lip.

"Maybe I should wait to test this ability any further until I know for sure that it will always work that way," he said.

She sighed, but wrapped her arms around his neck and gave him a light kiss, her fingers playing in the hair that was growing too long again at the nape of his neck.

"Okay. I want you to trust your ability as much as I do."

Her smile was radiant and he almost went back on his decision, but an errant thought made him grab her uniform and tug it upward with a big smile on his face and a kiss on her nose.

"What if this works for other people in the clinic?"

ZELLENDINE

THEY WEAVED THROUGH THE CROWD TOGETHER, HIS HAND IN hers, and she was thrilled to have the chance to watch Troylus try to heal someone.

But part of her was back in the wet room. Part of her wanted to return there with him and touch him until they were engulfed in blue light again. She didn't need healing anymore, but his ability was beautiful, and having it all to herself that way was like being surrounded by joy, until it hurt, but even then it was trying to do positive things.

In the clinic, they slowed, sedately walking through the rooms until they were in the one she thought held the patient who needed Troylus the most.

Last time Zellendine was in there, she thought the patient wouldn't make it. Burns covered too much of their body and they had to be kept close to stasis to avoid going into shock. It didn't matter how advanced their medicine was, some things were still impossible for them to cure or heal. Some things would kill one person while another would recover, and they never knew who would respond in what way.

He stepped to the bedside, wringing his hands in front of himself while she shut the door and locked it.

"But it hurt you and you were no where near this injured," he said, turning his silver eyes on her, his almost out of regulation hair close to hanging in his face again, and a muscle in his jaw twitched as he chewed the inside of one cheek.

"Are you sure this is a good idea?" he asked.

She stepped up to his side, taking both his hands in hers and kissing his palms.

"Troylus, you don't want to risk hurting anyone," she said, her voice hushed, "I understand that. But this poor person may not survive without you. And right now, they are almost in stasis they're so deep because their pain alone might kill them without that. They need you."

Letting go of his hands, she stepped back and put one palm between his shoulder blades so he knew she was there.

"If this doesn't work," he mumbled holding his hands out.

"Then they won't be any worse off than they are right now. But if it works, you'll have saved a life."

He took a deep breath she felt through his back. And before the blue light came, she knew to look for it, because his muscles bunched up, turning into rock hard cords beneath his skin that were so defined she felt them through his uniform.

Blue light, soft and hazy, different than it had been all other times she had seen it, swirled around the patient in a slow and breathtaking dance.

It seemed to go on forever and yet take no time at all for him to wilt, his hands dropping, and his legs almost giving out so he stumbled back into her.

"Are you okay?" She took him over to a chair where he dropped into it and leaned his head against her stomach.

"Sometimes, when I do too much, it almost knocks me out."

His words weren't crisp, clear, or loud, and she had to lean in to hear him and attempt to understand him.

"You can run out of power?"

"Um," he raised his head, although he was still leaning it against her and his smile was crooked. "I guess, yeah."

"Okay, let me run some scans. You just sit right here." She bent down and gently guided his head back so he was resting against the wall before she kissed him and turned back to the patient.

Through the bandages, she thought she could make out marked improvement in their coloring and less damaged skin, but she wasn't sure.

Scans sometimes took a while to show any change, and sometimes after the first few seconds, she knew some of her answers.

"It worked," she said.

"Huh?" he asked from behind her.

Darting back to him with the holo from the room in her hands, she pointed to some of the information on the scans as it came in, explaining to him what it all meant.

"So, they're going to live?" he asked, his face coming closer to normal and less like he was going to fall over.

"Yes, and other than the limbs they've already lost, and some minor scarring, they're going to be just fine." She tapped instructions into the holo to slowly bring the patient out of their pseudo stasis and pulled him to his feet.

"Let's go home, and get some sleep master medic," she said, kissing him long and slow.

His smile was radiant.

Walking out of the clinic, she had a hard time keeping her face schooled not to show the worried and sad people assembled there that she was thrilled. She just gave him the title of the assignment he had always wanted. And he had more than earned it.

Getting back to their quarters took longer than it had to make their way to the clinic, but that was okay with her. He held her hand, running his thumb over the back of it in slow, languid arcs. And every time he did, it sent a shot of energy through her.

Once they were in their quarters with the door to the hall shut, he grabbed her face in his hands and kissed her until she wanted to fall down.

He picked her up by her legs, wrapping them around his waist and carried her into the wet room. She dug her fingers into his hair, tangling it in her grip.

The door to the wet room slammed shut and he set her on the sink, his excitement clear to her through their uniforms. She pushed him closer with her legs behind him, the joy of him being with her making her forget for a moment about why they had stopped before.

But he bent his head and kissed the curve of her neck.

"Wait," she said, managing to remember there was a reason they had not pushed it before. "What about your ability?"

"Zellendine," he said, pulling back from her neck and giving her a wicked smile, "You just managed to have me drain my power supply."

"You—" He cut off her words with his mouth.

TROYLUS

AFTERWARD, HE TURNED OFF THE WATER OF THE WASH AND DRIED her off, his hands not wanting to stop touching her, wanting to make her cry out again.

"Just a fair warning, I don't know how I'm going to stop myself from depleting my power supply twenty times a day," he said, grinning and kissing her when she smiled, the towel bunching up between them.

"There isn't enough hours in the day for twenty times," she said and he laughed.

"I mean, I think we could try."

She kissed his nose and pulled the towel with her as she stepped away to put her uniform back on.

He dried off and followed her lead, although he was only half kidding.

Now that he knew the secret to getting to be with Zellendine however she wanted him was to spend all his ability on something, he would do it everyday. Somehow, he would find something that needed him to work on it.

"Zellendine," he said, leaning back against the sink, trying to find a way to ask her what he wanted, no, what he needed to know.

"Yeah?" she asked, running a comb through her long hair and looking over her shoulder at him.

"Do—" Nope. He wasn't sure he could do it. "What I mean is, you said you wouldn't partner until you were sure. And I know you said not until you were on the planet, but the planet is right around the corner, and…"

Fuck, how did people even begin to talk about this? There was so much on the line. He wanted to tell her how he felt more than he had ever wanted to do anything other than help her.

She put a hand to his cheek and he met her gaze. Those deep, dark eyes were soft and sincere. He was lost, drowning in them, and he didn't want to be found by anyone but her.

"Are you sure?" she asked, instead of answering him.

"Yes. Will you partner with me?" His voice was steady, but if he hadn't been holding onto the edge of the sink he thought his hands would be shaking.

"I want us to be partners." Her smile was brilliant and he swept her up in his arms, holding her off the ground and kissing her.

"Zellendine, no matter what, even if something happens that stops us, I love you." She had made whatever happened with leadership worth it, and he meant it. Even if they made sure she had to move on and find another person to partner with, at least he knew that right then, she wanted him.

"Troylus, I love you too, but nothing is going to stop us. I won't let it." She kissed him again, and soon they were back in the wash.

33

ZELLENDINE

SHE HAD NEVER BEEN SUCH A MIX OF EMOTIONS. THE PART OF HER heart that was broken over the loss of her father would never be whole again, but the rest of her, even the parts that were unsure and afraid of things, all of her was sure of Troylus. All of her was filled with joy at having Troylus want to partner with her.

For all their time in the wash, it was still awhile before Rullon came back to their quarters, and he didn't say a word when she and Troylus climbed into the same bed to sleep.

Wrapped around Troylus, his arms around her, her sleep was finally free of bad dreams.

The next day, he kissed her and left with Rullon to go to their assignment, but she stayed behind. She had to come up with some new idea, some new way to find out what happened to her dad.

Hours of tapping on her holo, thinking through what was near the small meeting room, looking for any other note from her dad on what he was doing there, she was no closer to an answer.

A chime rang out and an announcement called a series of names to come to the gathering room that evening.

Troylus's name didn't surprise her, the absence of Rullon's did, and so did hearing hers.

"Why do they want me? I'm not a starwalker," she mumbled to the empty room.

Maybe the gathering wasn't about the first spindles landing.

Once inside the gathering room, she stood to the side in the back and scanned the people assembled there, looking for a brown head of slightly too long hair.

Someone shifted and she spotted him, standing among other members of his crew, and a few starwalkers she didn't know.

His eyes found hers and his smile grew so pronounced, Parmita turned to look at Zellendine with one brow raised.

Parmita must have said something to Troylus because the people around them laughed and he smacked her on the shoulder as he passed her, heading to Zellendine.

Watching him make his way through the crowd, she wanted to be back in the wash with him, to be back in their private space away from so many eyes.

"Hey," he said, taking her hand and leaning to whisper in her ear, "if this is what everyone thinks it is, if we are both going on the spindles, I might jump up and down and cheer."

She laughed and nodded while he turned and tugged her through the room back to the group of people he knew.

"Are you going to be our medic, do you think?" Parmita asked, and Zellendine shrugged, but Parmita got a wicked grin on her face and went on, "Or are you just going to be with us to make sure he doesn't lose his shit from being away from you?"

Parmita put her hands to one side of her face and batted her eyelashes.

"Oh, now I see the Princess thing," Zellendine said.

Troylus cracked up, Parmita rolled her eyes and dropped her hands, but she was smiling.

"How long do you think they'll make us wait for this?" Troylus asked, looking around like he was trying to spot someone in particular.

"Leadership doesn't tend to want people to spend a lot of time without something specific to do." Zellendine squeezed his hand and he focused back on her, rubbing his thumb along the back of hers.

"Otherwise who knows what we would get up to," he mumbled into her ear while trying to play it off as him turning to look around them.

"Good grief. You two need to get this out of your systems before I'm stuck on the planet with you all the damn time," Permita said with a grin.

"You are going to be like this no matter what we do," Zellendine said. Parmita dropped her mouth open and everyone else laughed.

"Everyone," Alara's voice carried across the room, stopping conversations wherever they were happening and drawing all eyes to where she stood on the dais. "Thank you for coming. Look around you."

She moved her hands out to encompass the people crowded together, and a few did turn their heads from side to side, but Zellendine stared forward.

"These are the people who will be the first to step foot on our new planet."

A small murmur of excitement went up from the crowd, Zellendine and Troylus squeezed each other hands.

"You will be given your assignments regarding your specific spindles in the coming days, the computer will be making the decision regarding who will be assigned to which region."

"Region?" Troylus asked, the same thing she wanted to know.

"On this planet, like the last, we will have all seven spindles touch down at roughly the same time. Burghs will be set up around the spindles before some of those spindles return to the ship to bring more citizens down to colonize."

Alara still hadn't answered the question, everything was standard, as far as the little information shared with everyone when they were young.

"What will be different on this planet, is that it is larger, much more land to settle, and therefore the burghs will be much more spread out."

"No." The word came out of Zellendine in a rush of air as if she had been punched.

Troylus reached across himself to grab her hand with both of his.

"It will be unlikely that there will be much travel between the burghs for many years. The computer is taking all of that into consideration as it assigns each of you to your spindle. Obviously, we will ensure that all partners and all families share an assignment."

People around them were shifting and shuffling, everyone seemed to be as unnerved by the plan as she and Troylus were, but one word kept repeating in her head. Partner.

"Some of the regions we will be settling will require terraforming, in those places the spindle will return to the ship much later, or possibly not at all, and the other spindles will be put to use to transfer those citizens."

Which region was Zellendine going to be assigned to? Which was Troylus going to be assigned to? She wanted to march up to Alara and force her to tell everyone the most important piece of information. The rest of it was drivel. The important part was the assignments, and it was up to a shit computer that fucked everything up and was murderous? Zellendine inched closer to Troylus's side and ground her teeth to keep her mouth shut.

"Now, I want to congratulate you all for being part of the initial wave of citizens on our new planet." Alara clapped her hands and slowly the clapping spread, a few people cheered, and at least one whistled.

But Zellendine kept her hands in Troylus's, they didn't move an inch.

The second Alara was done, Zellendine squeezed his hand and let go, darting through the crowd to get to her before she left.

"Alara," she called, just as the older woman reached the threshold of the door.

But Alara must have heard her, because she stopped and turned to look back at all the people.

Zellendine popped out from between others and Alara's smile fell from her face.

"How are you?" she asked, no preamble and no small talk, just straight to the point about her tragedy.

"I would be better if I knew anything about a search for who did this to my dad," she said, which wasn't the way she wanted to start the conversation at all.

"Yes, well, I can't tell you the details, but we are doing what we need to. As for you, your focus should be to keep moving forward."

"Of course, but there is more."

Alara paused, her face betraying none of the annoyance Zellendine thought she would be feeling if the situation was reversed, but she also wasn't sure if she could trust Alara's calm exterior.

"Troylus and Rullon have been very important to my efforts to look forward. I would like to make a request to be assigned to the same spindle as they are." She held herself perfectly still, trying not to betray how much it meant to her for Alara to agree, while Alara tilted her head to the side.

"I would have thought you would wish to be assigned to the same spindle as Briar and his family."

"No. Briar and I will not be partners. In fact, I think he would appreciate if we were not assigned to the same region." Trying to keep her voice neutral, as if it was the same as any other falling out with someone, was more difficult than she thought it was going to be. Chances were high she was unsuccessful and Alara heard the anger in Zellendine's voice.

"Ah, I see. Well, I have little say in where the assignments are made but I will input the information into the computer to help it make its final decision."

She turned and walked away, leaving Zellendine to wonder why in the hell it seemed like Alara was lying.

34

TROYLUS

Zellendine was deep in her own head. All night and the next day, she was almost beyond his reach. More than willing to respond to his touch and go through the motions of conversations, she seemed to be star walking alone in the dark of her own mind the rest of the time. It was as if the meeting in the gathering room had sent her back too far into her own memories.

He tried to ask her about it, to find out what the conversation with Alara had been about, but Zellendine said she asked about her dad and had learned nothing. That wouldn't explain the amount of time they spoke or the way in which it was seeming to drive Zellendine to distraction.

After he was done for the day, he returned to his quarters, opening to the door to the smell of something crisp and sweet.

Inside, there was a branch from the orchard on the table, Zellendine perched on the edge of the chair next to it and some berries in some kind of creamy soup in a bowl on the table next to her.

"What is this?" he asked, dropping to crouch in front of her, taking her shaking hands in his and kissing her.

Her answering kiss was hungry and yearning.

"Zellendine," he said, trying hard to keep the frustrated growl out of his voice, "I was stuck inside trying to patch part of the floor today with loads of others to help."

"Ah, so maybe I should wait for the rest of this." She squinched her face, almost grimacing in what looked like an apology.

"No. What is this? It's fine." He tucked a piece of her hair back behind her ear and cupped one of her cheeks.

She closed her eyes, her face cleared, and she smiled.

"In a perfect world, I would be able to do this on the planet, or at least in the orchard in our clearing, but I want to make sure that this is just between us. So..."

Zellendine shifted in her seat and bit her lip, looking deep into his eyes.

"Troylus, I love you. I want us to be together on the planet."

"Me too," he said and she laughed while she put her hand on his mouth and shut him up.

"We talked about waiting, but I don't want to if it means we will be apart for years because we're assigned to different spindles."

He couldn't entirely track where she was going with this. It sounded like she was going to suggest they become partners before they left the ship, but that didn't make any sense. It had never been her plan, perfect world or not.

"Do you want to partner with me?" she asked, her bottom lip returning to between her teeth as his mouth fell open.

"You mean right away?"

She nodded and he put both hands on her face, searching it for any sign that she was doing this for any reason other than the threat of distance from leadership.

"Zellendine. I love you. I want to partner with you. But I want you to be happy. Don't do this because of them. I will find a way to get to you long before a few years. Trust me. Only do this if you want to."

Before he was even done talking, she was shaking her head and setting her jaw, her eyes turning hard and angry.

"Damn it, Troylus. I'm trying to do what needs to be done. If you don't want to ensure that they lose, then this is what we should do." She stood up from the table and stomped back and forth across the room.

"Is that why you want to partner with me? Because someone like me means they lose? What does that mean?" he asked, standing from his crouch on the floor and crossing his arms over his chest.

"That is not what I said," she yelled.

"Eventually, you'll see, they're trying to keep us apart. I just hope they didn't already succeed." She slammed the door to the hall behind her as she stormed out.

None of it made sense. How were they trying to keep them apart? And why would they care?

He sat down at the table, leaning against it with his head in one hand while he dipped a finger into the soupish berry mixture.

Putting his finger in his mouth, the sweet taste was the best thing he could have imagined for the moment he and Zellendine became partners.

Looking at the branch on the table, one that clearly came directly from the orchard, he spotted a little feather stuck among the leaves.

She had tried to make it perfect. She had tried to create a wonderful moment even though their entire ship was overrun with bodies. She had tried.

And he had fucked it up.

"I'm an idiot," he said to the empty room, jumping up from the chair so fast that it toppled over with a clamor.

Grabbing the door and flinging it open, he had to pull up short because Grandpa Kason and two of leadership's goons were on the otherside, the old man had a hand raised to knock on the door.

"Troylus, where are you off to?" Grandpa Kason asked, his eyes narrowed.

"I forgot something for Rullon. What's going on?" he asked, lying automatically although he couldn't imagine why they were there or why their presence raised chillbumps on his arms. It had to be about Stephen.

"Are you looking for Zellendine? Is there news? She's not here right now."

"Yes, there is news, and she doesn't need to be here for this. But you need to come with us."

3 5

ZELLENDINE

He was being an idiot. Fuck, why did he have to do this? Why couldn't he just say yes? Why did it have to be so damn hard?

Troylus wanted to partner with her, she wanted to partner with him, and she felt it in her gut that if they didn't do it soon, the Chapter was going to try and make sure they never got the chance to be that for each other.

She stormed through the halls, avoiding all the places that made her think positive thoughts of him, because she needed to keep hold of her anger or she would cry.

Under no circumstances could she go to the orchard, the damn cryo bay was out too. Even the clinic made her think of her dad too much.

It was strange that leadership would assign her as a medic to one of the spindles when she was doing her best to stay as far away from the clinic as possible.

Of course, if she thought about it, she realized it made perfect sense. She had no connections, no partner and no family. She was the perfect person to risk on the first landings.

If something was going to go tragically wrong, it would have been much less a problem for the rest of the population to keep moving forward if it happened to someone like her. She was expendable.

Fuck.

She stopped in the middle of the hall and leaned against a wall.

After a moment, she realized where she was, outside the terraforming office.

The orchard would have been better than there. At least in the orchard she was more likely safe than not, here it was the opposite.

She turned to dive into the crowd and head far away from there, but she ran into Briar, slamming against him and reeling back.

"What the fuck are you doing here?" He leaned into her face, his voice low and his mouth in a sneer.

Briar's silver eyes were exactly the same color as Troylus's, but his were cold, empty, and cruel, where Troylus's were soft, refreshing, and beautiful. Looking at Briar made her heart shrivel in her chest, the opposite of what looking at Troylus did. She didn't know how she had ever seen anything else in him.

"I'm allowed to walk through the halls. Get out of my way." Her voice was harder than she expected, none of the tremors threatening to show in her hands made their way out of her mouth.

"No. You are spying on me, aren't you?" He pinned one of her arms against the wall in a grip as tight as steel, it stole the breath from her lungs.

"The last thing I want to do is look after your sorry ass." She tried to wrench her arm free of his grip, pain shot up her shoulder and she gritted her teeth.

"You leave me alone," he said, his mouth next to her ear. "Just be happy all these people are around."

His other hand shot out, fisted up, it slammed into her stomach, doubling her over, and he let go of her arm, slamming her into the wall with his entire body as he walked past her.

It took minutes that seemed like hours for her to be able to get to her feet and walk down the hall again.

Along the halls back to her quarters, she wondered if she should even go back yet, if Troylus had forgiven her enough for them to have a conversation again.

She laughed to herself, dark and humorless. Maybe he would be too upset to try and heal whatever damage Briar had done to her arm and shoulder that caused sharp pain to shoot through her with every step she took, and to her stomach that ached and throbbed.

Whatever the Chapter was going to do, whatever spindle they were assigned to, she had to make sure Briar wasn't with them. She doubted she would survive if he was.

Opening the door to her quarters she was met with Rullon standing over a toppled chair, his arms crossed, and a shaking hand over his mouth.

"Rullon?" she asked, tears already welling up in her eyes although she didn't know why. "Where's Troylus?"

"He's been accused of Stephen's murder."

36

TROYLUS

"You know I didn't do this," he said, his head back against the wall, his knees pulled up to his chest in the tiny closet that was his holding place.

"We have reason to believe you did. A witness has come forward," Grandpa Kason said from the other side of the door.

"A liar has come forward." Troylus took a deep breath and wished he had a way to tell Zellendine he was sorry.

Now he knew why they shouldn't be partnered. He shouldn't be partnered with anyone. The Chapter recognized something within him that they identified as a threat. He should have known. That show in the gathering room was just to make him think he was finally going to get something he wanted from them. But instead, he was locked up, and going to be put into stasis permanently.

There was a shuffle on the other side of the door, not that it mattered to him. Not unless they were bringing Zellendine and Rullon to say goodbye.

Fuck. Even that, he wasn't sure he was capable of saying goodbye to them.

She was going to be so angry, so hurt. He rubbed his hands over his face and silently asked the universe to keep her from doing anything that was going to get her in trouble or wounded. At least she was going to the surface. At least she was going to be okay. Rullon and Parmita would look out for her on his behalf.

"If you need anything," the honeyed voice of Alara floated through the door, it lacked any of the sharp edges of Grandpa Kason's. She almost sounded concerned, but that had to be a play. She was just as much leadership as Grandpa Kason. She had to be as supportive of the punishment as everyone else was. "Someone will be out here for anything you need, including a trip to a wet room. We will be moving you to permanent stasis in a few days when we are able to clear out the halls and a cryo bay at the same time."

Ah, so they were waiting until the launches of the spindles. That was the only time they could possibly expect everyone to be clear of where they wanted them to be. It would be real easy for leadership to funnel all the people who wanted to watch into certain places, and tell all the rest they weren't allowed certain places for a short period of time. It made sense during the launch. Every other time, people would have questions.

"What's the matter, Alara? Aren't you proud of this fucked up decision made by leadership? Shouldn't you be showing off your prisoner?" He banged his head back against the wall. Even his taunting sounded tired and worn.

She sighed, a heavy and drawn out sound.

"Troylus, none of us want this to happen."

"Yeah, sure." He laughed, the sound devoid of humor.

"Maybe, if you tell us how you did the damage and why, maybe we can find a way to help you join back with the other citizens eventually."

"If I was the one who had killed Stephen, I would tell you.

But since I'm not..." He shrugged and shook his head at himself because no one could see him shrug.

"Just think about it, Troylus. It would be a way to get out of permanently being in stasis." Her voice was heavy with meaning, but she may as well have been speaking in made up words, because what the hell was she instructing him to do?

"Are..." he stopped, and she coughed, letting him know she was still there, "Are you suggesting I lie?"

His voice was a whisper, hoping the slats in the door were enough for his voice to carry to her.

"I am suggesting, that answering the question could be very beneficial to you." There was a shuffling and flurry of sound moving off into the room.

She was. Alara was suggesting he lie.

ZELLENDINE

"Rullon, he didn't do it," she said, pacing back and forth in the small patch of floor between the table and the door in front of the bunks.

"I know he didn't. But Zellendine, they think he did." Rullon righted the chair and sunk down into it, his head in his hands.

"So, how do we prove he didn't?"

"He doesn't have anyone to vouch for his whereabouts. He was just wandering the halls. Unless someone noticed him. And how would we be able to find the people who did, among everyone, that would be willing to come forward?"

"No one even knows this is happening. We have to get the word out. Someone had to have seen something."

"People won't be comfortable, they'll think it's looking back. We're so close to getting to the surface, no one wants to risk their ride to the planet." He raked his hands through his hair, leaving tufts of it standing up. It reminded her of Troylus's too long hair when it got mussed up.

An ache opened in her chest, more acute than the pain from Briar's attack.

"If we can't get the people to do the right thing, we have to figure out which silver-eyed person has the ability to create fire." She stopped in her tracks, thinking through what little they knew of the abilities.

"Troylus fixes things," she said out loud, her thoughts creeping out.

"Yes, that's basically what starwalking is. It's in space, and dangerous, but it's fixing things," Rullon said, staring off into space and clearly not paying attention to where her mind was. But he was right.

"Rullon, starwalking is fixing, and the ability Troylus has is fixing. So, who would have an assignment that would make sense with developing a fire ability?"

His head popped up, his eyes wide, while his mouth worked open and closed.

"I... I don't... I don't know," he stammered, but she knew he was thinking like she was now.

She pulled out the other chair and sat across from him, pulling out a holo from their station.

The list of assignments that popped up reminded her that she didn't know all of the different crews onboard. When they were learning, they went over them all, but there were too many to keep track of.

"Help me hide the ones that wouldn't make any sense. We'll keep it big picture. Maybe some will only barely make sense, but we keep them as possibilities." She started eliminating some of the crews on the list and handed it to Rullon who went through and deleted more from their list before he shook his head and handed it back.

"Stasis is an obvious no, but engineering and service? I mean, maybe," he said, scratching his head and looking out to the middle of the room while she scanned the list again.

"Medic is out, but what about robotics?" she asked, rubbing

at her forehead where a headache was forming. This was taking too long.

"Here," he said, gesturing for the holo.

She handed it back to him and tried to think through what she knew about the systems that robotics used, and if they would necessitate knowledge of fire at any point.

"And what about the kids? Upton is turning silver and I think his ability is something with the mind, something almost prescient. It's weird." She shook her head at the words coming out of her mouth. They were talking about people with incredible abilities and she was describing Upton's cryptic comments as somehow more weird than Troylus remaking reality.

"The attack on your dad wasn't done by a kid. It was too well controlled. It didn't happen in the middle of the hallway or at the clinic. It was someone conniving, and I think they did it on purpose. Hmmm." He tapped on the holo and squinted, then stared off into space.

"What about terraforming? They deal with fire and heat and climate," he said, his brow furrowed.

Rullon seemed unaware that she couldn't breathe.

Zellendine stood up from the chair, her hands braced on the table in front of her, her shoulder and arm screaming, her stomach aching, and the hole in her heart ripping open further. But every broken and wounded part of her was filling, knitting itself together with rage.

"I know who did it."

Her voice was harsh and ugly, Rullon snapped his eyes to hers.

"Briar killed my dad."

38

TROYLUS

Before being locked up, he didn't know there was a wet room off the gathering room. The only benefit of his situation was the size of the wash. He could lay in the water for hours, letting it fill to his shoulders and luxuriate in being more engulfed than he had ever been.

No trickling, tiny amount of water meted out over time while he got colder and colder in there. For leadership, in their secret wet room, it was all the things he had always wished he had in his own quarters.

Apparently they thought it was okay for him to know how much they were holding out on everybody since he was going to be frozen forever.

He closed his eyes and allowed his head to slide under the water. Somewhere in the inner workings of the ship, after he was done, the water would be processed and used again.

Maybe, before she left for the planet, his water would find its way to Zellendine and they could have one last wash together while they pretended they weren't both wishing for a bed.

In his mind, he imagined a life with her where they had their own quarters, no matter how small. Just their own space to be together and not worry that at any moment his dad could walk in on them.

Banging sounded on the other side of the wet room door.

"Go away. I'm not done," he yelled to whoever was enough of an asshole to interrupt the only thing he got to do.

"When you are finished, I will be here," Alara's voice answered. Even while yelling through a door, her voice was melodic and it pissed him off.

No one who worked so hard on behalf of leadership should be gifted with that beautiful a voice. It made it a lot more difficult to hate her, and almost impossible not to listen when she spoke.

He tried to get back to the place in his mind where he was living with Zellendine, where he was happy and free of the Chapter and all their regulations and stupid mottos. He tried to make his way back to the warmth of the water soaking into his body. He tried to not be aware.

But none of it worked, even the warmth of the water was starting to fade, the cold sinking back into him.

Swearing under his breath, he pushed the button that opened all the drains and in seconds he was standing in the center of an empty wash, dripping.

Drying off was quick, but the cold had sunk into his bones by the time he was done and back in his uniform anyway.

Maybe it was good he was chilled all the time now, soon he was going to even more frozen.

His own dark humor wasn't even funny to him anymore. That probably wasn't a good sign, but then again it didn't really matter.

That actually did make him smile as he finished drying his hair.

Alara was standing on the other side of the door, her hands in front of her and her face serene.

It made him want to punch a wall that she was so happy.

"Why are you here?"

She turned to him and her smile morphed into one of sympathy.

"You should be given every opportunity to tell us all that you know."

"No. There's still nothing I know about Stephen's death, or anything else. Put me back in the little hole. I'll sleep standing up again for a while." He walked over to the door of the tiny box of a closet.

It didn't matter how much he did not want to be back in there, it was safer than being in the large gathering room if any member of leadership was around.

"Troylus, I don't want you to go into stasis. All your crew members value you, and what you have managed to do for Zellendine despite the differences you have with her, it's all commendable."

He didn't respond. She had made it clear that she wanted him to come up with something, anything. There was no promise that even if he did it would change his fate. So why would he risk doing something to make life worse for someone else?

"No, thanks. I don't want to talk to any of you. I have few hours left, I would rather it be spent thinking about the people who I will never get to see again."

She flinched. The unflappable Alara, who he wasn't sure until that moment was entirely human she was so perfect all the time, flinched.

"I..." She let her voice trail off and looked down at the floor for so long he started to think she was going to just walk away instead of finishing her sentence, but eventually she looked up at him again. "Maybe I can get you a chance to see them."

His traitorous heart skipped a beat and thudded as fast as it ever had in his chest. He wasn't sure he could take seeing Rullon and Zellendine again, but even the thought of it made him feel warmer and more alive.

Troylus nodded before one of her helpers opened the door to the closet and he climbed inside.

39

ZELLENDINE

"You don't know that," Rullon said, shaking his head.

"He's attacked me twice," she said, trying not to be embarrassed by it, even as he reared his head back and jumped up, coming to her side and looking her up and down like he would be able to spot her injuries.

"Neither time were his abilities involved, he used his fists and his feet. Once he used a table."

"Shit."

Zellendine barked out a laugh even though it wasn't funny, but she shoved the sleeve of her uniform up her arm to expose the clear bruises forming in lines that coincided with where his fingers had been.

"That little asshole," Rullon said.

"You're not wrong. But some of the things he was saying made no sense, and now I think they were all about him killing my dad. The problem is that I have no idea how to get anyone to believe it was him, let alone how to bring in someone who could cause the kind of damage he did to my dad. No one wants another accident."

Rullon wandered around the room, not quite the marching style pacing she had done, and not in her back and forth pattern, but close. And she couldn't help wondering how she was going to keep him from getting hurt.

"So, how are we going to get Briar to tell on himself? That has to be the way we go about this," Rullon said, finally coming to rest back in his chair, leaning forward on his elbows on the table.

"You're right. That would be the best way, but I'm not sure how to go about that yet. I do know that I feel like I need to speak to Upton. And no matter what, I'm getting Troylus out of there." She curled her hands into fists and wished, not for the first time, that she had some kind of ability so she could use it to help them.

"Upton is tiny. Why bring him into this?" Rullon frowned, his jowls growing more pronounced.

"Because, I think he already knows. I think he was trying to warn me the last time I was there, I want to know what else he might know." She took over walking the room, going back to her pacing instead of taking up the circuitous path Rullon was wandering.

"Do you think it might help us trap his brother? And do you think you can even get in to see him without a big problem with his brother?"

She wasn't sure she could avoid Briar in the attempt, not unless she had a way to know he would be somewhere else.

Zellendine was facing the door as the idea struck her, she stopped mid step, her foot falling unceremoniously from the air to drop to the floor, her momentum over. She turned around slowly to look at Rullon.

"Are you willing to help me? I don't think we have a lot of time to do all we need to. The spindles are supposed to be heading out soon. And Troylus is going to be on one."

"First of all, of course I'm going to help. I'm trying not to be insulted right now that you thought you had to ask me. But second, how are you going to get Troylus on a spindle if this doesn't work? We don't even know where they've got him locked up," Rullon shook his head like he didn't believe she could do it, but she meant what she said.

"I'm not heading down to the planet unless he's going to the planet too. And I know exactly where he is. You forget, I've been the one in trouble."

Watching the memory of her trial come to his mind was like watching as the Wheel turned so she could see their sun out a window.

"Rullon, do you see the dessert in front of you? And the branch?" she asked, taking a seat at the table across from him and gesturing to the sad remainders of the special moment she had planned.

"Yes, I just had bigger things to worry about than why Indigo would have dropped off something from her work," he said, shaking his head and narrowing his eyes like he thought she was missing the point of their entire conversation.

She smiled, of course he would have thought the branch was because of Indigo.

"The orchard is a special place for Troylus and I, and I made that dessert for him because I was going to ask him to be partners with me."

His eyes widened and then crinkled at the corners as a giant smile grew on his face. All of the joy on his face was gone in a matter of seconds as the reality of the place they were currently in crashed against her news.

With a nod, Zellendine said, "Now you know how much I mean this, if I can't get him let out, I'm breaking him out."

"Zellendine," Rullon's face turned into a sad version of the smile that first overcame him at her news, "I'm so glad he has you in his life. But I need you to make me a promise."

Her immediate reaction was to say yes, anything. She wanted to make Rullon happy and to do whatever to honor him that Troylus would want her to. But under the circumstances, she didn't trust him not to do the dad thing and trap her into promising to stay out of it.

She bit her lip, but nodded.

"Please, try as hard as you can to stay away from Briar. I don't trust him to be anywhere near you. I don't want you to get attacked again. I don't think Troylus would forgive me if we get him out just to have you end up in the clinic. Or worse."

There was no good way for her to answer that. Yes, she was going to try not to get her ass kicked by Briar again, especially since she doubted he was capable of, or even wanted to hold back his power. If it was a matter of face down Briar, or get Troylus out, she was more than willing to step in front of Briar's fists.

But she nodded, because he only asked her to try. And that she could agree to.

"Okay, so here's what we're going to do."

40

TROYLUS

HE WAS FOLDED UP ON HIMSELF.

Trying to find a comfortable position in the damn closet was going to drive him to actually want to go into stasis. His anger was even starting to flare up again.

Just irrational fury at all the people who weren't in there with him. Not Zellendine like before, but all the other people.

It made him wonder if he needed to use his ability or it would it build up like pressure until it was more likely to just pop out and run rampant.

But what would be the worst thing his fixing ability could do? If it could have fixed him up some leg room, now that would have been useful...

He shoved against the wall and tried to get his feet under him, twisting and turning and thumping against the walls trying to stand up in the skinny box.

One of his feet were asleep, it made the whole thing more complicated and it felt like he hurt his ankle more than once because of the bizarre way his asleep foot was barely working.

"What's going on in there?" One of the big watchers on the

other side of the door yelled through it at him, banging on the wall next to the door.

"Nothing, trying to get comfortable in this damn hole," he yelled back, grinding his teeth together as he tried to be quiet while he got to a basic standing position without too much weight on the side with the worthless foot.

Leaning his head against the wall and his butt against the opposite wall helped to alleviate some of the pressure. Slowly, the pins and needles grew to a dancing party of prickles all the way up to his ankle bones. The whole damn thing had lost all feeling.

No matter how much trouble it had the potential to get him in, he had to do something. This was ridiculous. And some poor asshole after him would eventually be inside there again. Leadership was way too happy to punish, in his opinion.

The real question was, what was behind the walls, what could be moved to make more room for his body.

He shoved some of his ability at the wall, nothing happened, he shoved harder, the blue light growing brighter.

But it wasn't expanding the area in front of him, it was sliding down the panel to the floor and moving things there.

What the fuck? The words almost slipped out of his mouth, he expected the whole wall to move, but his ability apparently had a better idea. Although he wasn't sure he agreed.

Finally, he let go of the light. It left him tired, there was so little energy left in his body from shit sleep and stress.

Sliding down the wall, it was awkward to crumple himself up in order to slide into the tight fit of the space his ability had made for him. But he did fit. It was as if the wall continued in a small box, just the right size for his body.

He stared up at it, the section above him close enough to his face that if he sat up he would smack his nose on it long before he was upright.

It was good enough. Maybe it would help him get used to the idea of being trapped inside a cryo tube for eternity.

Maybe not.

But it was enough for him to close his eyes, make a wish for Zellendine and Rullon to be safe, for them to know he was as okay as he could be under the circunstances, and fall fast asleep.

41

ZELLENDINE

SHE WAS TUCKED AROUND THE CORNER, HIDDEN BY THE CROWDS that still filled the hallways.

The door to Briar's quarters opened and he stormed off.

Good, he got Rullon's message.

Making her way to his door seconds after he left, still only gave her the equivalent time it took for Briar to navigate the halls to the starwalker office and back if he didn't want to stay and talk for very long with Rullon.

It didn't take long after her knock for Upton to open the door.

"Hi, Zellendine. Everyone is out right now, but Briar will be back soon," he said, prancing off into the room.

She made her way inside and shut the door, thanking the universe that it had worked out better than she hoped for, even if she only had a few minutes.

"That's okay, I'm here to see you. How are you feeling?"

"Much better, but I still have bad spells like Pop says. Dad says I need to be careful not to let too many people know." He climbed onto a chair and perched on the edge of it, grabbing a bar from the table. Master of subterfuge the little guy was not.

"Well, I'm happy it's bothering you less."

He nodded, smiled, and took another bite.

"Upton, can I ask you some questions about what you told me before?"

Shifting in his seat and looking around the room like someone was going to jump out and get him in trouble, he finally nodded.

"You know I'm in danger."

He nodded, his little face looking more grave.

"Can you tell me, without having a bad spell, do you know if my dad was in danger in the same way?"

"Yes, he was. Not as much, because he was more like us than you are, but he still was."

She still couldn't entirely understand what 'like us' meant to him, but it didn't matter as much as getting to the point.

"Do you know who hurt my dad?" Her voice was quiet, but by his reaction she knew coming to see him was worth the risk. It was as if another explosion had gone off.

He dropped his bar, pieces of it scattering across the table, and his little hands shook as he wrapped them around his knees and rocked back and forth while he shook his head and closed his eyes.

"Upton, I'm sorry to bring it up. But Troylus is being blamed for it."

Eyes open and staring at her, tears welling up in them, he started keening. A quiet sound, undulating high to low and back again, his mouth remained closed and the sound filled the room with a haunting quality that almost made her flee.

"Listen, you don't even have to say anything. I don't want you to do anything you're uncomfortable with."

The keening stoppped, but the tears were still ready to fall and he kept rocking.

"Was it someone I know that hurt my dad?"

He nodded, the rocking slowing. This approach must have been easier for him to handle. She wondered if he was more afraid of the truth he held, or more afraid of speaking when his ability might come out.

She wanted to not need to ask him. She didn't like doing this to him, to make him get so close to things he feared. It felt too much like she was attacking a child. But Troylus needed her to keep trying to figure this out. Even if she still felt a need to send a wish into the universe that her dad would have understood. Although she didn't think he would have approved.

"Upton, I am sorry I have to ask you any of this. I'm sorry that your ability is hard for you."

Wide eyes blinked at her and his mouth popped open only to slam shut almost immediately.

"Yes, I know about the abilities. Although most people don't. My dad was trying to understand them when he died. I really need to know if it was Briar who hurt my dad."

She didn't ask it as a question. She stated it as a need, a fact that she already suspected and just wanted him to tell her if she was right. To take as much of the weight of a decision to tell on his brother from him, to hopefully make it less painful for him.

He stared at her for long minutes, not even rocking anymore, just still and staring.

Finally, he shut his eyes, a single tear escaping to trail down each cheek, and he nodded his head.

Protocol wasn't ready for moments like this. She crossed the room and kissed the top of his head.

"I'm sorry, Upton. Don't worry, I won't ask anymore questions, and neither will anyone else. I won't let anyone know you told me."

He sighed and she left.

Nothing good could come of her spending anymore time with him. Her very presence seemed to trigger his ability, and she knew it was hard for him to be as brave as he was.

She hurried from their quarters, making her way along the hallways, away from the main path to get to the starwalker office. Hopefully Rullon would still be there, because she wasn't sure she could go back to their quarters and sit alone with the information.

Ducking around the corner, Parmita spotted her from the area by the airlock and raised a brow.

"What are you doing?" Parmita asked, coming to her side.

"Is Briar still in the office?" Zellendine asked.

"Yikes, the break up was that bad, huh? No, he left a few minutes ago." Parmita gestured with her head toward the hallway leading away from the office on the other side.

"Thanks." Zellendine took a deep breath and made her way into the office.

"Oh," Rullon said as soon as she was passed the doorway, he folded over and rested his head against the table in front of him. "Let's not split up too much for a little while, okay?"

"Why? What happened?" She squeezed herself against the wall as other starwalkers kept going about their business and she felt like she was in the way.

"Is this her?" One of the others in a chair asked Rullon gesturing to Zellendine. She didn't know the lady's name, but the question only made her more worried about what Briar had done while he was in there.

Rullon nodded and the woman whistled.

"Stay away from that guy," she said, turning to Zellendine with wide eyes and a shake of her head. "He has some serious issues with you."

"I know." The last thing she wanted to do was go through the many reasons why she knew, she still had aches in her arm and abdomen to prove it.

"Did you get confirmation?" Rullon asked, his words careful even in the room full of people who would have supported them trying to clear Troylus.

She nodded. There was no point in saying anything, it was enough.

Rullon slumped in his chair, he didn't look relieved, and she wasn't really either. Yes, she knew for sure, and she had never believed it was Troylus, but still. A friend, someone she had once wanted to partner with, had killed her dad. Even if it was an accident, and she wasn't sure it was, that ache in her heart was only worse for knowing.

"Fuck," Rullon mumbled, earning him a sidelong glance from the lady next to him who had no idea what they were talking about.

A commotion started in the hallway and people in the office sat up to attention.

She turned to see what was going on.

People moved out of the way to reveal Alara standing in the doorway.

"Hello, Rullon, Zellendine, I'm glad you're both here."

Rullon glanced at Zellendine, and she shrugged. Her plans didn't include a visit from leadership.

"Can we help you with something?" Zellendine asked, her voice more acidic than she expected, but it wasn't like Alara didn't deserve it.

Alara nodded, her face resigned.

"Yes, I would like for you to come with me and speak with him."

Rullon jumped from his seat, but Zellendine put out a hand to stop him from rushing forward.

"What's the catch?" Zellendine asked.

Alara turned the same appraising look on Zellendine she gave her when she reported to leadership about the wombs and the loss of Yanna and Anders's baby.

But this time Zellendine stood up straight and stared back.

"There is no catch. I only want him to be able to see you before he is put in permanent stasis."

Every molecule of air left her lungs in a whoosh, she grabbed onto Rullon's hand, not sure who was holding up who.

"Permanent…" She couldn't finish the question. She couldn't even process what it meant. She didn't think she would ever be able to say it out loud.

"Unfortunately, we don't have a good alternative for this sort of action," Alara said, casting her eyes to the floor.

"The sort of action he didn't take. You know this isn't him. You know he didn't do this," Rullon said, his voice gruff, harsh, and loud.

Other people in the room shifted in their seats, but Zellendine was finally able to take another clear breath. Alara wasn't answering Rullon. She was struggling to make eye contact. It was all Zellendine needed to know.

Plans formed in her mind. She wasn't going to let leadership take Troylus and put him on ice, not for any length of time, let alone forever.

"Lead the way," Zellendine said.

Alara's eyes snapped up to hers, a line showing between her brows. Rullon turned to look at her, but he squeezed her hand and let go before turning his face, suddenly more angular and rigid, toward Alara. The other starwalkers went silent as they passed on their way to see one of their own. And if Zellendine's plan worked, save him.

42

TROYLUS

Knocking on the door of the closet woke him up from the best sleep he had managed since he was locked up.

"What?" he mumbled, not wanting to squeeze himself out of the cramped sleeping space unless he had to.

A scream, muffled a second later, rent the air and bounced off the hard surfaces around him causing a weird reverb he thought sounded like Zellendine.

He scrambled to get upright. The possibility that he was about to have something worse happen to him because he used his ability to get some damn sleep made the blood run faster through his body. Even though he couldn't imagine what worse would be.

Troylus slammed his head against the corner of his little space where it met the regular wall and started swearing.

"No, everything is fine. Stay out there. We need time," Rullon yelled.

Rullon?

Doubling his efforts, Troylus finally got to his feet and on the other side of the open closet door stood Zellendine with her hands over her mouth and Rullon shaking his head.

He no longer felt the place he smacked his head, he threw himself into their arms, wrapping one of his around Zellendine and one around his dad.

"Why are you here? Are you both okay?" The last thing he wanted was for either of them to end up in the same position he was in.

"Alara said we could see you," Rullon said, patting Troylus on the back and leaving a hand on his shoulder as he stepped out of his embrace.

He understood how hard it must have been for his dad to even maintain that level of contact after a long life of the protocols. And it broke his heart he wouldn't be with Rullon when they were on the planet and finally free of the restraints that had defined their lives.

"Zellendine," he said, bending down and kissing her forehead as she clung to him and cried, her shoulders shaking, "Why did you scream?"

She laughed and said, "I thought they had chopped you up and I was looking at what was left. I've been in that closet before, I know there isn't room to lay down like you were."

"Well, you didn't have my ability to make yourself a weird little space to sleep in. See? I'm okay." He ran his hand down her back, her long hair running through his fingers, never wanting to let her go.

"You're going to be okay," she whispered, heavy emphasis on the word going. She lifted her face to his and put a hand to his cheek, her smile was wavering but her eyes were as determined as he had ever seen them.

Rullon nodded, patting at Troylus's shoulder.

"Don't," Troylus said, looking at each of them, the thought of them being in his position making his stomach drop into his toes. "Whatever you're doing, I don't want you to get in trouble like me."

"I will do what I need to. I love you," she said.

"And you're my kid." Rullon shook his head, a wry smile on his face. "No chance of me sitting this one out."

"What's your grand plan, then? Find the real killer?" he asked, with a small laugh.

Zellendine smiled and kissed him, a kiss he had missed so much and knew was so precious and few that tears built up behind his eyes.

She pulled him to sitting on the floor with her and his dad with them in a tight circle.

"What would you think if I told you we already know who the real killer is?" she asked, threading her fingers through his.

"How? And have you told leadership?" Did he have a chance to get out of this? His stomach picked up from his toes and shot into his brain making him light headed. But it only lasted a second before he caught the glance Zellendine shot his dad.

"No. We don't have proof yet, but we'll work on it. And we have other plans just in case. There is no way we're letting this happen to you when you don't deserve it and we're so close to real freedom and a real chance." She ran her other hand along his arm under his uniform sleeve like she couldn't get enough of touching his skin which he had to agree with. But the rest of her statement made him shake his head.

"Listen, I appreciate you both trying to help, but I mean it when I say I can't handle it if you lose out on that chance because of me." He patted his dad's hand with one of his own and then moved it back to run his fingers through Zellendine's hair that he pulled from behind her to drape over her arm.

"Troylus, even you can't stop us. We will figure out a way, don't give up. If it comes to it, we'll need you to be ready,"

Rullon said, his voice low and his eyes glancing over to the main door of the gathering room.

"How did you manage to get them to leave us alone for this? I mean, seeing me is more than I expected them to actually do, but letting us talk privately is..." Troylus shook his head. It was fucking bizarre and unbelievable without a catch is what it was.

"I asked Alara what the catch was." Zellendine sighed and climbed into his lap, wrapping her arms around his neck and laying her head on his shoulder.

"And? What was the catch?" he asked, resting his cheek on the top of her head.

"She said there wasn't one. I think she feels bad." Rullon frowned, his jowls lengthening because of it, but he was looking off into space, when he turned to look back at them, he smiled. It made him look younger, and Troylus hoped he would have a long life ahead of him still.

"Will you be filling me in on who the real killer is? Or is it safer if I don't know?" His voice was incongruous with what he was saying, he sounded like he was talking about a really tasty dessert, not a killer framing him and getting away with it. But it was hard to be as angry as he should have been when he was sitting next to his dad and had Zellendine in his arms.

Rullon looked at Zellendine and she nodded against his shoulder.

She lifted her head and her face was a mask, blank, it made him wonder if she was trying to prepare him for bad news.

"Briar. I think Briar killed my dad."

If he had been standing, his legs might have given out. It was one thing for Briar to be a big enough asshole to physically hurt Zellendine when he was in the throes of the silver change effect, but to kill someone? Stephen of all people? Troylus wanted to hunt him down and beat the shit out of him.

"How was I so wrong about him?" Troylus mumbled, and Zellendine laughed.

"Tell me about it."

"Oh, Zellendine, I'm an idiot," he said, pulling her to him and kissing her, then putting his forehead to hers, "I'm sorry."

"I am too." She shut her eyes and he kissed her again.

They outlined the plan for him in hushed tones and a lot of touching, none of them wanted to look back on that chance and regret not taking full advantage if things didn't turn out well.

Alara opened the door to the meeting room sooner than anyone wanted her to, and none of them bothered to hide their physical closeness. What was being scolded for breaking protocol when they were all looking at permanent separation?

She sighed when she saw them, but she didn't say anything about it.

"You know he didn't do this," Zellendine said, and Troylus closed his eyes, burying his face in her hair.

Of all the things he would miss, she was the one that he couldn't get enough of. They had been afforded so little time.

"Do you know," he said, brushing a piece of her hair away from her face and tucking it behind her ear, "You're the only person I've ever loved. For a while I thought I would never meet someone I really wanted to partner with. But you changed that, and I love you."

Zellendine sucked in a shaking breath, he knew she couldn't say the same, but it didn't matter to him. She loved him now, and that's what mattered to him.

"You know I love you. And you know I'm sure," she said.

"That's all I want." He kissed her, the love and sweetness of it mixing with the salt of both their tears.

Rullon helped him stand up, offering him a hand and pulling him into a hug, his shoulders shaking while they held onto each other.

"Just," Rullon said, patting his shoulder as they pulled apart, his mouth working like he couldn't form the words.

"I know, Dad." Troylus nodded and Rullon took a deep breath before he stepped back, wiping at his eyes.

Tears poured freely down Zellendine's face, but she looked serene and strong when she held his face in the palms of her hands and kissed him, deep and hard and then soft and sweet. The whole pantheon of kisses she gave him in the seconds she had.

All he could give her back was to envelop her in a hug and kiss her forehead before he turned and closed the door of the closet behind him. The last thing he could handle was watching them walk away.

It didn't take work for him to curl into a ball and lay back in the cubby hole he had created for himself, his legs could no longer hold him up anyway.

The sound of the gathering room door swinging shut let him know he could choke out the wracking sobs waiting in him.

He wanted to believe they would be able to do what they were trying to, that they would save him from his sentence. But part of him thought the Chapter was too big and leadership too big an obstacle.

Of all the things he wished his ability gave him, he would have traded the chance to sleep somewhat comfortably in the tiny closet for the ability not to doubt.

4 3

ZELLENDINE

SHE STUMBLED INTO THEIR QUARTERS, RULLON RIGHT BESIDE HER and just as unsteady.

They both collapsed onto their bunks, neither of them saying a word.

With only so much time before she was to be sent off to the planet, she knew she should be trying to put her plan into place, but she could barely move at the moment.

It might have been an hour, or a few hours later, her tears finally ran dry.

Not long after that, Rullon asked from his bunk, "Do you want me to make something from the service?"

"Yes, thank you," she said, staring at the wall at the back of the bunk.

"Zellendine..."

The hesitation in Rullon's voice made her roll over and sit up to look at him.

"I want you to know, that if this doesn't work—"

"It's going to work," she cut him off. She didn't want to even begin to accept the other possibility. There was only one way she wanted to spend her life, with Troylus. Anything else wasn't worth imagining.

"Okay. Well, I just want you to know that no matter what, you will have us. I'm going to let Indigo know, so that after I'm gone, you'll always have this family as your own." His face was set, but his eyes were soft as he stood next to the service, paying no attention to the food he was preparing.

All she could do was bite her lip and nod.

He smiled, a small smile that managed to tell her he was happy she accepted and that he would always feel the hole left by Troylus as much as she would if they were going to be in that empty situation for any reason.

It wasn't until he turned and got back to his task that she got her voice under control enough to say, "Thank you."

The night before the spindles were scheduled to launch, during one of the busiest times in the halls, she tucked herself along a wall, hidden by the people walking by. She watched, even though she couldn't hear anything, while Rullon approached the two people posted at the door to the gathering room.

His hands waved in the air, those passing near him squeezed further into the others in the crowd, giving him as wide a berth as they could.

One of the men at the door stuck out a hand like he was trying to usher Rullon away.

But Rullon smacked the extended arm down.

The other man went to step in, then Indigo got involved, emerging from the crowd.

Zellendine remained in place until Rullon and Indigo drew the men away from the door, gesturing wildly, their faces red and livid while they continued to yell.

She darted along the wall while the crowd was distracted and slipped into the gathering room.

It took seconds to sprint across the room and fling open the door to the closet, it was still unnerving to see just a section of Troylus's torso and the top of his legs.

"Come on," she said, "Time to go."

He climbed out better this time than last, he was at least awake and expecting her, but she was bouncing out of her skin by the time he managed to get out of the closet and grab her hand.

They didn't have the time for a proper hello, but she gave him a quick kiss and ran with him to the door.

Opening it a crack, she peeked out, and the people in the hall were still distracted by something she couldn't see off to one side, although she knew it was Rullon and Indigo giving the men hell.

She pulled him along behind her, back into the crowd along the wall just the way she came, but she took the first corner into a different hall.

The second he was around it behind her, he tugged her back into him and wrapped her in his arms for a too swift hug while he whispered, "I love you," in her ear.

"I love you too, now move your ass," she said, weaving into the people with him, hoping they would blend as well as she planned for when she came up with her untethered idea.

Making their way to the spindles and hiding him onboard was the only chance they had, and she just had to make it work, they just had to get there without being spotted.

Through the halls they went, no one even looked at them.

She wondered if he was going to get too tired and start slowing after so long not using his legs enough, but they were going fine. And they weren't pushing their speed so much they would stand out. Maybe their path to the spindles was going to be okay. Maybe her plan was going to work.

But making another turn, getting even closer to their goal,

she almost ran right into one of the only people onboard who was for sure going to notice them.

He jumped back from her, shoving her backward into Troylus, who caught her before she could tumble to the floor.

Briar stared at her, his lip curled in a snarl.

"Sorry," she said, stepping to the side, and attempting to pull Troylus along with her.

"No. But you're going to be," Briar said, shoving her as she tried to get past him, sending her careening into the crowd.

"What the fuck, Briar?" Troylus yelled, earning him a shove in the other direction.

All she could do was try and get Briar to focus back on her before it registered with him that Troylus was there. Only then could she worry about getting them past him before it got any more likely they would be caught.

She made eye contact with Troylus who was bracing himself like he was about to kick Briar's ass, and she shook her head.

The crowd started to clear, squeezing together to give them space for whatever disaster was about to happen.

"Briar, come on, I'll go away and you can go the way you were heading. You have to be going somewhere," Zellendine said, trying to get away from him and being herded further away from Troylus in the process.

She cursed herself when she realized she had managed to get backed up against a wall with no one around her and Briar was between her and Troylus.

"Fuck you." Briar's voice was loud and guttural, like he went from zero to ready to rip her head off in half a second.

'No, thanks, not from you,' was what she wanted to say, but she had to clench her teeth together and remind herself she couldn't afford the mistake of making any of it worse.

"Just let me go on my way," she said and he snarled.

"Why? So you and the escapee can go ruin something else?" he asked.

She shot a panicked glance at Troylus and focused back on Briar.

"Oh, you thought I didn't know? Who do you think turned him in?" He wasn't even quiet about the confession. He was loud and proud about being a horrible human being to someone who used to be his friend.

There was no more biting her tongue, she knew, the only option was confrontation and running.

"You fucking murderous piece of shit. He's better than you in every way and the day I figured it out is the best one of my life," she said, wishing she had an ability so she could hit him with it.

He screamed and ran at her, punching her in the stomach and doubling her over.

Troylus pulled him off before he could get in another blow, they twisted and punched until they threw each other with enough force that they separated. They still ended up close to their original position.

"Leave her alone, Briar," Troylus said, wiping a split lip.

Briar was bleeding from a cut to his eyebrow, but he didn't even seem to notice, he turned back to Zellendine with hate in his eyes.

"Did you see that? You did that?" Briar yelled, pointing at Troylus.

"You're the one who destroyed your friendship with him, just like you're the one who killed my dad."

44

TROYLUS

"Briar," Troylus screamed, terror and horror flooding through him as Briar sent a ball of flame flying at Zellendine's head.

At the last second, she darted just out of the way, her hair getting singed on the ends in the process. She rolled along the ground and it seemed to put it out.

But his scream drew a derisive sneer and flame filled look from Briar.

"Stop this." Troylus braced his feet and lifted his hands, if Briar attacked him, he wasn't going to pretend he was defenseless.

"Oh, I've been wondering," Briar said, his voice a mockery of glee. "What can you do?"

"More than you fucking think. Leave her alone." Troylus wanted to just punch him like he would have back before Briar switched shifts and both their eyes changed colors.

"You know, I don't really believe you. I mean, you're a star-walker. It's the job for the useless and everyone knows it. The most likely to die, the least valuable." Briar formed another ball of flame and threw it at Zellendine, she ducked and it whizzed over her head to land among the crowd that scattered as it neared them.

"The most important," Zellendine said while Troylus cursed her in his head. She should have just stayed out of it. He could keep Briar distracted. "Because otherwise the ship would have broken a long time ago. You know that. You're just an asshole looking for a way to hurt someone."

"Zellendine," Briar said, tsking. "Now that's not nice."

"What's not nice is attacking me, and what's down right evil, is killing my dad."

If Troylus had not been paying attention to the smallest flicker of movement from Briar, he would have missed the tiny flinch and the way his eyes darted to the side away from her before returning full of even more hate.

"Fuck. You did kill him." Troylus dropped his hands to his sides, his mouth falling open.

"Both of you are too fucking stupid. I've done nothing wrong."

"Amazing." Troylus lifted his hands again, his sadness over what Briar had become burning away and being replaced by white hot rage. "You really think you did the right thing."

"No. Briar, how… how could you think that?" Zellendine's voice was low and hollow as she slumped to the ground and stared at Briar, opening herself for attack.

What the hell was she doing? Get up, Troylus shouted in his head, afraid that if he drew any more attention to her position it would make Briar more likely to throw fire at her, not less.

"Of course I did the right thing," he yelled, throwing his hands in the air and laughing, the fire ball popping out of existence. "Does everyone hear this? She thinks her traitor father deserved to live."

"My dad was a member of leadership, not a damn traitor you

zealot." She sat up straighter, drawing Briar's hateful attention again.

"Then what was he doing sneaking around, Zellendine?" Briar's arms erupted into flames, the fire licking all the way up to his shoulders, but not burning his uniform.

How it did that, Troylus had no idea, but he didn't drop his hands, and he sure as hell wasn't going to.

If she was going to make herself a target, offer herself up as the object of Briar's rage, then his hands and his ability was his best chance to stop her from dying in front of him.

"Sneaking around?" She was screaming now, her own anger seemed like it was winning against whatever plan she was trying for. "That's your evidence that he had to die?"

"You don't know." Briar's voice cracked and his fire grew, his uniform beginning to smoke, threads of it floating up and turning into flaming wicks in the air.

"Neither do you," Zellendine said, her voice had gone from as hot as Briar's fire to as cold as space. "You killed him for an assumption only cooked up by your irrational hate and anger." She stood as tall as she could stretch, her whole body almost vibrating with the force of her own fury.

"What were you going to do, just let Troylus take the fall for you?" She wouldn't stop, she leaned forward and took a step even closer to Briar, closer to the danger.

No, fucking stop, what are you thinking, he wanted to scream at her, but he thought it would only make things worse. He shook his head, trying to get her attention and make her back away.

"Troylus is probably guilty too." Briar's voice shook, but it didn't make him sound scared, it made him sound like he was about to lose control of his emotions, and his power, completely.

"Briar." She didn't lose any of the steel and ice in her voice, but now it was laced with an insidious and almost more toxic level of pity. "You need to get help from one of the medics. This isn't good for you."

"You are a sanctimonious piece of shit. We will never be friends. You were just using me." His fire had engulfed his entire upper body, his head was barely visible through the flames.

"Using you?" She looked past him, making eye contact with Troylus, holding position with her hands at her sides and her nose in the air, her back straight and tall.

He prepared himself for whatever was going to happen next.

"For what?" She asked, each word carefully articulated, and Briar reared back, a massive fireball forming in his hand.

Time slowed for Troylus, just like it had when he remade the window and when the accident happened. The only thing in the world he was fully aware of was the specific situation in front of him and how he was going to manage to make his ability save everyone, not just Zellendine this time.

Briar twitched, and that was enough. His fireball flew from him toward Zellendine, and the crowd just behind her.

She shut her eyes, the people behind her only had a second to start to move.

His hands flung out and pulled.

The walls, floor, and ceiling peeled. Parts of each tore off and wrapped around Briar and scooped in most of his fireball, enclosing it in with him in a metal and wood mass, centered around a screaming Briar.

Zellendine lifted an arm and flinched away. The remainder of the fireball slammed into her upraised arm and set her alight.

45

ZELLENDINE

SHE SCREAMED AND ROLLED ON THE GROUND, THE INFERNO smothered against her own body, which she knew would put it out, but it didn't lessen the pain. She was pretty sure it made it worse, like it was driving the fire deeper into her.

By the time she got the flames out and was sitting on the floor, holding an undamaged part of her wrist and whimpering, Troylus skidded to her side.

"Oh, Zellendine," he said, kissing her forehead and holding his hands over her arm, he shut his eyes and his blue light poured out of him, wrapping around her wounds.

It made her arch her back and grind her teeth so she didn't scream. She managed that, but there was no keeping the groan in, even though she knew it was going to hurt.

The pain ricocheted up and down her arm and spread into her whole body.

Troylus let go of the light, stopping it and the sensation of tearing that was ripping through her in a second.

He looked at her with a smile and toppled over.

"No, Troylus," she yelled, picking him up off the floor and putting his head in her lap.

"It's okay. Just drained," he mumbled, so low she had to lean down to hear him, and then his eyes were shut and he was out.

"Shit," she said. There was no way she was going to be able to get him to a spindle before someone came along.

Her arm wasn't completely healed, and what was better was still bright pink. Her uniform was shredded and burned most of the way up to her shoulder, allowing the patchwork skin of her arm to be visible to the entire crowd in the hall that were circling her and Troylus, and the collection of random ship parts that contained a screaming Briar.

"Will he throw fire at me too?" A young girl asked her dad, pointing to the pile of crap.

"No," Zellendine said, from her place on the floor, the girl and her dad turning to look at her, other people around doing the same. "He can't get his ability through all of that stuff that Troylus surrounded him with."

Several people let out large breaths, their shoulders relaxing, and the girl kicked a foot out at a piece of wood sticking out of the bottom.

"Killer. You should stay in there," she said, and Zellendine had rarely agreed with anyone more.

"What in the universe?" Alara said, picking her way through the torn up floor and eyeing the mound of stuff while Briar screamed from inside.

"That guy," the young girl said, pointing at the wailing mass, Briar's words were distorted and warped so by the time they came out they were just unintelligible noise, "is bad."

A smile tugged at the corners of Alara's mouth as the young girl spoke.

"He killed that girl's dad, he said so. And he wouldn't even say sorry." Alara snapped her gaze to Zellendine on the floor with Troylus in her lap, and Zellendine was surprised to see no shock on Alara's face, just more assessment.

"Then," the little girl went on, her voice heavy with meaning on then, "He threw fire at her, twice. Once it hit her and burned her arm."

Alara made her way to Zellendine's side, looking closely at the patchy skin of her arm and the burnt up edge of the shortened sleeve of her uniform.

"That guy," the girl pointed at Troylus, "Closed the bad guy up with stuff, and healed her arm, although it looked like it hurt, then he died."

"Died?" Alara asked, looking up at them both before she leaned closer to Troylus.

"He's not dead," Zellendine said, smiling at the girl and her very succinct summary, "He did too much with his ability and he passed out from exhaustion."

The girl smiled and tugged on her dad's arm, pulling him away from the scene.

"Ability?" Alara asked, her voice hushed when the girl was gone.

"Silver-eyed people, which there are more of everyday, are developing abilities. The accident that happened?"

Zellendine didn't want to say it, she was worried how the people with silver eyes would be treated if all of leadership deemed them dangerous, but she had to warn people now that the basics were out in the open.

Alara sighed and closed her eyes for a second before she shook her head.

"How did we not know about this?" she asked.

"The same way you didn't know that Briar killed my dad." Alara raised her eyebrows and Zellendine had to deliberately temper the anger in her voice. "You didn't want to know. We didn't understand what was happening to Troylus, but we knew you would think of it as a threat no matter that all he does is fix things."

She stared at Zellendine for a moment, but finally slumped her shoulders and nodded, because even she had to admit it was true.

"Why did Briar attack you and your dad, though? He was close with you both."

"Because the ability first comes along with some weird rage that Zellendine is a unique trigger for," Troylus said, his voice weak and small, but there.

"Hey," Zellendine said, brushing his hair out of his face even though his eyes were still closed. He smiled and remained as still as before.

"So, is Briar to blame then or not?"

Troylus did open his eyes at that point, his smile falling into a grim line.

"Yes," he said. "I had the same rage at Zellendine when my eyes first turned, but I made a choice not to let it win. Because it is really clear, even in the middle of it, that it's irrational. Briar didn't make that choice. He needs to face some consequences. But not stasis forever." He shook his head a fraction, as much as her lap would allow and shut his eyes again.

"Why not stasis forever?" Alara asked.

"Because it's cruel," Zellendine said, putting her hand on Troylus's cheek and wishing it was what she wanted. But in reality, she wanted Briar to go away and never bother anyone again, while it was Troylus who thought of the cruelty.

Troylus, she decided, was a better person than she was. And she was okay with that.

Rullon and Indigo came around the corner, being led by the two guys who had been posted at the door.

"Let them go," Alara said, shaking her head.

Indigo rushed over to Troylus and relaxed when he opened his eyes, Rullon took his time, a smile on his face.

"He over did it?" he asked, sitting down next to them.

"Of course," Zellendine said.

While Troylus caught them up on everything, he gained enough strength to get up from the floor. And all of them walked back to their quarters, not looking back at the mess that was Briar's cage even once. Leadership could handle Briar, it wasn't their problem anymore.

46

TROYLUS

Waking up with his arms wrapped around Zellendine and hers around him, was sweeter than he even remembered it being.

For a split second, he wondered if he would have appreciated it as much if he hadn't thought it would be gone, but he dismissed that idea.

There was going to be no stupid attempts to see the good in the bad about the utter shit situation he had been in. No, he was just going to do what had been drilled into his brain since he was tiny, keep moving forward and try to forget.

He buried his face in Zellendine's neck, deciding it was his favorite way to wake her up as she started to squirm and tangle her fingers in his hair.

"You are going to be really hard to live with on the planet, huh?" she whispered in his ear and he laughed into her neck.

"Not for you. For everyone else, probably," he said with a wink and kiss.

"Okay, you two, big day today." Rullon climbed from his bunk with a big grin on his face and made his way to the service. "Have you checked which spindle you're on? I need to know what time you're boarding so Indigo can come see you off."

"We're on spindle 4," Zellendine said, kissing Troylus again before she climbed from the bed and headed to the wet room.

"Let me check what time we'll be boarding," Troylus called to Rullon and checked his schedule on his holo.

But it didn't say he was assigned to spindle 4, it said he was assigned to spindle 1.

"Shit," he yelled, jumping up and throwing things on.

Rullon came out of the service with his eyebrows high, and Zellendine stopped to cock her head to the side as she walked out of the wet room.

"What are you doing?" she asked.

"Going to find Alara and have her switch my assignment to spindle 4," he said, reaching for the door.

"You're not with me?" she asked, grabbing his arm.

"I'm on spindle 1."

Rullon groaned, but he held up a hand, stopping them both.

"Okay," Rullon said, "So, they did the assignments before everything went to shit. We'll eat something after you both put in emergency meeting requests on your holos. After yesterday, they have to listen when it's you two. Then they'll fix it when they get here. Come on, don't freak out."

Troylus still wanted to get it taken care of right that second, but his dad had a point. It was their last day on the Wheel, they shouldn't spend it stressed and not with Rullon and Indigo.

He pulled Zellendine into him for a hug, and did what his dad asked.

Indigo and her partner showed up not long after they sent their messages and ate with them while they all speculated about the planet, the timeline for the rest of the population to land, and all manner of other things.

Rullon could have told them stories from when he was young on their last planet, but he still had trouble looking back. Plus, Troylus thought it was more fun to imagine all kinds of possibilities and he thought Rullon agreed.

Not long after they ate, there was a knock on the door.

Troylus hopped up to answer it, holding it wide open for Grandpa Kason and Alara on the other side who nodded their greetings to everyone inside.

"You received our messages?" He asked, not bothering with small talk.

"Of course," Grandpa Kason said, "And we would like to accommodate your request, but I'm afraid we can't. Not at this late date." But the smile on his face and the frown on Alara's, told him that was a lie.

"Why not?" Zellendine asked, coming to stand next to him, her arms crossed over her chest. "I'm sure one of the other star-walkers or medics would switch with one of us."

"Because we didn't give anyone else the option to choose who they were assigned to a spindle with, we can't play favorites," Grandpa Kason said, his smile brighter.

"No," Rullon said from behind him. "Since her father died, she's been living with us, she's become like a member of the family. All families were supposed to be assigned together."

"Like a member of the family could be said by a lot of people, I'm sorry but that doesn't work."

"If you hadn't locked me up, we would be partners by now," Troylus said, and Zellendine slipped one of her hands into his, threading their fingers together.

"That happened fast, it was just last shift that you were furious with her," Grandpa Kason's smile didn't slip, but his eyes narrowed.

"I told you about that," Alara sighed, "It's complicated."

"Zellendine, Troylus, I'm so sorry," Alara said, turning to

look at them and boxing Grandpa Kason out of the main section of the doorway. "I was out voted. But, as soon as the spindles start to deliver more colonists to whatever burgh you're in, there will be travel allowed between them, and you can re-settle at one of the others after you're partnered."

Grandpa Kason and Alara nodded and left.

There was no more to do, there wasn't a way to stop it.

He was going to be separated from Zellendine.

She flung her arms around his neck and hugged him tight. He wrapped his around her and held on.

"No matter what, I'm making this as fast as possible, and getting back to you," he said.

"You better," she said, pulling back so she was looking in his eyes, "I'm going to miss you."

They kissed, what he knew was going to be one of their last kisses for what could be a year. It was too much time. Somehow, he was going to have to come up with a way that he saw her sooner than that.

All day spent with his sister, her partner, his dad, and Zellendine, wasn't enough when they had to split up to get on their spindles. It wouldn't have been under normal circumstances, but after his time locked up, it wasn't even close.

But they said their goodbyes, they made their promises, they shared their awkward pats on the back, and their passionate, if melancholy, kisses, and they split up to their individual assignments. Onboard the Wheel, or on two different spindles, they separated to start the biggest change year of their adult lives.

47

ZELLENDINE

She ran the number through her head again. It was the most important thing she owned. The knowledge of how to spread the word.

They may have taken away her father's holo, made sure it stayed in the clinic, but they would never think to look in that file. They would never realize exactly what she had. And they would certainly never realize that it didn't matter that they had taken it, other than it pissed her off even more.

Maurice next to her, suspended as she was in straps, bounced a little. His grin was gigantic, and his eyes wide, although there were no windows on the spindle.

Rullon said he was a friend, so she tried to stay next to him. The one person on the spindle she felt like she could trust at all, was someone whose name she had only spoken for the first time the day before.

For a guy who seemed pretty solid attitude wise, and who was closer to Rullon's age than hers, his bouncing made her feel like she was strapped in next to Upton.

"Excited?" she asked, smiling despite herself.

"Of course I am. Planetside... It's been way too damn long. You're going to love it." He pointed his grin at everyone, making eye contact with each of them.

Some of the people around them smiled back, even if shyly, some just opened their already wide eyes more as if his enthusiasm was scaring them. But one person, a girl with a bright yellow tie in her hair, flipped him off with a wry grin.

Zellendine laughed. A sound she was unaccustomed to in recent days.

But it felt right to laugh on the way to the planet. It felt right that she was about to be as free as she was going to get.

As soon as everyone else made their way down from the ship. As soon as she found Troylus, got him back in her life, whether at her spindle or his, and anyone else who wanted to leave their settlements behind, she was going to send the message. And then, she would really laugh.

4 8

TROYLUS

OF ALL THE WAYS HE IMAGINED HIS TRIP TO THE PLANET TO GO, and there had been so many over the years, including the ones where he didn't go at all, none of them were quite like this.

The straps over his shoulders and crossing his chest felt too flimsy for what they were about to do. But he couldn't look to the side and joke with the person next to him about it. He didn't know them.

He didn't know anyone on his spindle. Not a single person even looked familiar to him from the faces he had seen in the halls or starwalkers who worked similar hours.

In every scenario he had conjured up in his mind, someone he knew was part of his landing crew. But the other starwalkers were from different shifts. The terraformers were none he had ever even seen. And the medic wasn't her.

Maybe it wouldn't have bothered him so bad if she was staying behind. Which sounded shitty, even inside his own head, but if she was still on the ship in the clinic, he could believe she would eventually be assigned to his same burgh and join him. But she was in another spindle.

Not for one damn second did he believe the computer chose their assignments. Not for one damn second did he believe that it just happened to put Zellendine in a spindle as hard for him to get to from his as possible.

But if leadership thought their little game was going to end with them on opposite sides of a damn mountain range and not with them broadcasting their information out to the other ships, they were in the wrong universe.

As the spindle shifted around him, separating itself from the others and the Wheel itself, moving through space toward their new home, he made the planet a promise.

Someday, even if it took him a year, he was going to make a home there for him and Zellendine. He was going to do it away from the Chapter, their computers, and all of their lies. He was going to do it with her help and create a place where any of the people who didn't want to be part of the main group could find a community.

He just had to figure out how to get to where her ship was. He just had to land.

EPILOGUE

Briar

ALL HE HAD EVER WANTED WAS FLYING OFF. WITHOUT HIM.

He watched out the window of the gathering room, the view split by cobbled together pieces of metal and lots of sealer, while people around him celebrated. But there was no joy in him seeing the spindles depart. Not when he wasn't on one. Not when it wasn't a mission he should have been a part of.

Those people didn't know what it was like to care about being a good citizen of the Wheel. They didn't care. They wouldn't have done what he did. They wouldn't have done what was needed. But they got rewarded.

And all he got to do was watch and stay silent. Grandpa Kason had made it very clear that no one else would understand, and he wasn't to say a word. But he wanted to. Oh, he wanted to.

He wanted all of them to be stuck on the Wheel and for him

to be the one to set foot on their planet first. He wanted to be the one to claim it for the Chapter.

But instead, he watched as the daughter of a traitor, the one who had probably looked backward and was probably in on the plot with her father to take down the Chapter computers, flew away.

The only thing left for him to do was look forward. Look forward and plan.

AFTERWORD

Thank you for reading!
If you enjoyed this book, please leave a review at your favorite
book vendor.
The third book in The Grimm Star Saga: First Light
is called
The Shattered Aurora
and it will be out soon!
While you wait, don't forget to check out the other books by the
author, get a free book, and keep up to date on all the upcoming
titles at
jdarleneeverly.com

ACKNOWLEDGMENTS

A whole hearted thank you to Bean, the Rottens, and all of my friends and family. A big bag of thanks again to Jupiter Alley and Magnolia editing for their help in making this happen, as well as the team at Wishing Well. This story kicked my butt, and then it picked me up off the floor and dusted me off, more than ready to write the third book for Troylus and Zellendine. Trust the muse, for she is wise, and if you don't listen, she'll still win.